Thrill Seekers

Erotic Encounters

T0317990

mischief

Mischief
An imprint of HarperCollins*Publishers*
77–85 Fulham Palace Road,
Hammersmith, London W6 8JB

www.mischiefbooks.com

A Paperback Original 2013

First published in Great Britain in ebook format by
HarperCollins*Publishers* 2012

Copyright
Under the Big Top © Kathleen Tudor
Cabaret Girls © Olivia London
Shining Knight © Flora Dain
FHAFH © Elizabeth Coldwell
Cerise Calls It 'Research' © Giselle Renarde
Pulparazzi © Heather Towne
The Portcullis © Rose de Fer
Making It Work © Tenille Brown
Park and Ride © Victoria Blisse
The Arrangement © Cèsar Sanchez Zapatae

The author asserts the moral right to
be identified as the author of this work

A catalogue record for this book is
available from the British Library

ISBN-13: 9780007553402

Find out more about HarperCollins and the environment at
www.harpercollins.co.uk/green

CONTENTS

Under the Big Top
Kathleen Tudor

'He's still watching you,' Kris' best friend whispered. They both giggled, a little loosened up by the wine they'd been drinking and the unusually lively atmosphere of the bar.

'He's cute,' Kris whispered back. The guy in question had been sitting across the bar watching her for about ten minutes, and grinning at her every time she glanced his way. Melanie had tried winking at him, but he'd only smiled politely at her and moved his eyes back to Kris.

'You should go talk to him.'

'No way! I can't just walk up to some random guy!' But when Kris tried to sneak another peek at him, the cute guy was gone and a serious-looking couple was taking the table he'd been sitting at. 'Damn, he left,' she said, surprised at how disappointed she felt to be potentially missing out.

Melanie giggled and then slipped from her stool,

something about the bathroom coming out mangled by her mirth. And as she vanished into the crowd, Kris' mysterious stranger dropped onto the vacated seat and toasted her with his glass.

Kris moved automatically to touch the rim of her wineglass to his, inhaling the scent of whiskey as she used the gesture as an excuse to lean closer. 'Fancy seeing you here,' she said, a flush of pleasure rising in her.

'I'm Daniel,' he said. 'You from around here?'

'Yeah. You're not?' She withheld her name on purpose, a tease for making her wait soth= long before he approached. Daniel … she liked strong names.

'I'm with the Candy Apple Circus. We're in town until Tuesday.' He drank off the rest of his whiskey and eyed her in an obvious challenge, or maybe he was just waiting for her to fawn.

'I'm Kris,' she said, shifting her posture to give him a better look at her breasts. 'What do you do in the circus, Daniel?'

'Strong man act,' he said, and it was good that he was grinning, because otherwise she would have accused him of being a bad liar and walked away. 'Or maybe I'm an animal tamer. Or the ringmaster himself …'

'Or a clown?' she teased.

'Definitely not a clown. I think those guys work harder than anyone else,' he said, and he surprised her with his sincerity when he said it.

Respect for the clowns, huh? She believed that he was with the circus, at least. No one else would have thought about that, although once he said it she could believe it. After all, they had to do all of the running around and jumping through the whole show, not just one act.

'So not a clown, and not a strong man. Maybe you shovel elephant poop.'

'No elephants,' he said, laughter in his eyes. 'We have horses, but I don't shovel their shit, either. Does it matter what I do?'

She shrugged her shoulders and he sighed as if put upon.

'All right then, I am an assistant tent master. That giant tent that has to go up and come down fast and perfect every time we move. I help make sure it happens. And that it doesn't collapse the first time somebody hops up and down in the rigging. You can feel free to brush me off now that I've told you what a boring job I have.' He made a comically exaggerated wounded face, and Kris couldn't help but laugh.

'Okay, so it's not as exciting as trapeze guy …'

'Trapeze guy! Why didn't I think of that? I could be the Flying Daniel!'

She laughed again as he struck a silly pose. 'It's still pretty cool. You must get to see a lot of cool places.'

'All over the states,' he agreed. His fingers found hers on the bar, and she let him take her hand. 'But the tent is home once you let it get under your skin. I could show you.'

She'd seen circuses before, but there was something about being able to see it when the tent was quiet and the lights were out that made her shiver with anticipation. She liked to see things behind the scenes, quiet, with the make-up off and the defences down. She'd been backstage at a television show, once, and the actors all out of character, with their make-up off and their hair a mess had been a revelation to her, and strangely exciting.

'I want to see,' she said, and stood with him, letting him pay for her wine along with his whiskey.

She hesitated for a minute when he led her to a beat-up looking truck in the parking lot, but his smile was sweet and disarming. 'It doesn't look like much, but it tows great,' he said. She got in.

The approach to the tent was much as she expected, but the real excitement was driving through the gates off to the side and behind the tent. There, dozens of trailers and motor homes sat parked in neat rows, generators purring. He pulled into a dirt lot filled with cars and mostly trucks, and she was so stunned by the intimacy of the sight that he had time to come around the truck and gallantly open her door for her.

'Are you going to get into trouble for this?' sheg. this? asked.

He shrugged and winked. 'Not if I don't get caught.

4

Really, though, there are only a few people who would mind, and they're all asleep at this hour. Come see.'

Kris tried to take in everything as he led her toward the huge tent. She was hungry for it all, and the sight settled in her belly like a glow of arousal, awakening other kinds of hunger. She took a breath outside the canvas, savouring the moment, then he lifted a flap of the tent and gestured her forward, and Kris stepped into every child's dream.

The tent was nearly empty except for one man standing in the centre of the ring. She stepped forward with Daniel as the man levitated off the sawdust floor of the centre of the ring, and she realised that he was holding on to some sort of gymnastic rings. 'Probably Jake,' Daniel said, not bothering to lower his voice. Kris stepped forward to get a better view.

'Probably?'

'They're a twin act, Jake and Josh. But Josh tends to spend his evenings in more carnal pursuits.' 'Probably Jake' was contorting himself into some pretty impressive shapes, every muscle in his arms bulging as he suspended himself gracefully above the ring floor. He moved through the poses slowly and with control, and the surreal performance in the empty circus tent made Kris feel like she had stepped into a dream.

'It's amazing.'

'I think they're Family. You know, get born into the

circus, trained to balance on the high wire as soon as you can walk, sort of thing.' The act apparently ended, and 'Probably Jake' lowered himself gently to the ground and took a bow toward the centre of the ring, then toward the seats before straightening and turning to his impromptu audience.

'I'm going to go out and find Josh before he gets himself into too much trouble again. Goodnight, Danny,' he said. He turned and gave a bowing sort of greeting to Kris, then left through the same flap they'd come in.

Daniel put an arm around her waist and guided her to a small, protected cove beneath the risers. 'This is where me and the crew stand to watch some nights. It's got a great view of the action,' he said, speaking low and right into her ear. The vibrations of his voice sent shivers down Kris' spine, and she leaned into him.

'Like your own secret clubhouse. Can I see the stage?'

'The ring. Come on.' He stepped forward and offered his hand, leading her out from under the risers and forward, over the raised ring that captured the performance area and into the centre of the ring itself. He let go of her and she moved around the ring slowly, taking in the amazing backdrop from behind which the performers would emerge, the lights and rigging above her, and the rows and rows of empty seats. They seemed focused on her, expectant, and she had a powerful urge to do something magnificent to fill them.

'It's amazing,' she said. He sat on the raised platform that went almost all the way around and she went to him. That hot burn deep in her belly was growing hotter than she could stand, and she wanted to thank him properly for showing her something so marvellous.

Daniel pulled her close to him and swept his tongue over her lips, and she opened for him, allowing his kiss to pass deep inside her and tease at the fires in her belly. She could almost hear the echoes of cheering and applause, and instead of driving her to hide, it made her want to give all the more. She pressed forward, easing over him until Daniel was lying on his back on the two-foot-wide platform and she was lying over him, a smile curving her lips. His hands rested on her waist, and she kissed nd, she kihim again, letting her body press down into his.

'This place is really incredible,' she whispered to him. He smiled and stroked his hands up and down her sides.

'And I get to build it from scratch all over again every time we move. How cool is my job, now?'

'Very damn cool,' she said with a laugh that surprised her. She caught his bottom lip between her teeth and bit down gently, and he moaned and pressed his hips up into hers, showing her the extent of his enjoyment of the moment. 'So where would you bring someone backstage if you wanted to have sex with them?' she asked into his ear.

He shuddered beneath her before he answered. 'Oh,

I wouldn't do it backstage. Backstage is a royal mess, with make-up and costumes and props all over the place. Someone would probably end up with a juggling pin up their ass or something,' he joked. 'Most people would just go back to their trailer or a sleeper car or something and that would be that. But if I wanted to do it in the tent, I'd do it right here in the middle of the ring.'

She laughed lightly and nipped at his neck. 'Would you?'

'Oh, sure. The bigwigs who would be really pissed are all dead asleep this time of night, and it's great in here. Sheltered. Clean.' He tucked his hands behind his head and watched her.

'What if someone walks in?'

'What if they do? Trailers don't exactly have sound-proof walls. I think we've all pretty much heard everyone else going at it at one time or another, so no one's really shy about sex around here. Unless *you're* shy, of course.'

Kris rolled her eyes, but the desire welling up in her – inspired as much by this place as by the sexy and surprising man she found herself with – was impossible to ignore. She could insist they get into his truck and find someplace quiet to go neck, but ...

She leaned forward and kissed him again, letting some of the heat inside her out to sear him, too. Then she stood up and wiggled out of her tight top, letting it and her bra drop into the ring. She leaned forward again, and he sat up halfway to meet her, his hands finding her breasts and caressing them gently, kneading and squeezing and leaving her wanting so much more. His mouth moved over her throat and she moaned and pressed into him.

He sat up and pulled her to him, and suddenly she was straddling his lap and his mouth joined his hands on her breasts. 'Harder,' she gasped, and he bit down hard enough on one nipple to make her want to come right then and there. She must have made a sound that he approved of, because he immediately moved over to bite down on her other nipple, too. She gasped as the pleasure washed over her, a hot coal bursting into flame and warming her whole body with pleasure. She gripped him tightly, pulling his head toward her body and fisting the back of his shirt with her other hand.

Then he tipped his head back and smiled at her, and the sweet boyishness of that expression made her kiss him on the forehead, the cheeks, the eyes, and finally on the lips. She let the tenderness and pleasure she felt spill out of her into that kiss, her tongue caressing and sweeping through his lips. She teased and tasted him, and let him to do the same to her, embracing the power of a mere kiss to both satisfy and enflame. He was gentle and patient, stoking her fires and using his hands to tease the naked flesh of her back and ribs.

'I bet you take all the girls to kiss under the big top,' she teased, and by the way he laughed, she'd caught him by surprise. She sucked his lip into her mouth and kissed him again before he was forced to repipsorced tly, not really wanting to know if she were the first or the fiftieth woman he'd brought here. Tonight, the magic of the tent belonged to her, and she wrapped herself in it like a warm cloak.

Her fingers found the buttons to the front of his shirt, and she didn't break the kiss as she started to unfasten them, letting the slow rhythm of the buttons be their own sort of tease. She let her fingers dance over his skin more than they strictly had to, took her time with each button, and teased a little in between, but soon she ran out of buttons to unfasten, and his shirt came down over his shoulders and away.

He was tanned and healthy, his muscles well cut and gorgeous under his shirt. It had also hid a tribal tattoo that went across one pec and partially up over his shoulder. She turned her head to examine it, letting his lips fall to her neck to continue their exploring there as she traced her fingers over the edges of the design.

'This is beautiful,' she said, surprised by the art.

'I found my tribe when I came here,' he said, placing kisses along her collarbone in-between his words. 'These people are my family. We're nomads, but we stick together, take care of each other. That's rare nowadays.'

'I can see the appeal,' she said, leaning forward to let her tongue trace the path that her fingers had just taken.

He moaned as her tongue traced the lines on his hot skin, and when she got to the top of his shoulder and bit down, his arms tightened around her and he gasped.

This time it was him moving over her as he pushed her gently back, lying her down on the narrow wooden platform. He kissed his way down her body and stopped at her pants, his hands on the clasp but his eyes on hers. She nodded and he unfastened them, pulling her pants and panties away and dropping them and her shoes off to one side. She expected him to shuck his own pants and climb on top of her, but he leaned forward instead, lying on his belly and greeting her sex with a hot lick.

She moaned softly as he tasted her, thrusting his tongue in deep and then licking softly at her pussy. He sucked one of her lips into his mouth and teased at it with his tongue before pulling away and giving the other side the same treatment. He followed the trail of her moans, repeating the things that pleased her and phasing out anything that didn't get much of a reaction until she was half-crazy with arousal, her hips bucking up into his mouth against her will.

She turned her head and a moan caught in her throat as she caught the eye of one of the performing twins. He'd come in on the opposite side of the tent, perhaps, and was standing under the risers, half-hidden and unobtrusive, watching. She remembered how he'd left shortly after they had come in and wondered if he had known what was going to happen here tonight, or even if he and Daniel had planned it that way.

But then Daniel sucked her clit into his mouth and her mind went blank with white-hot pleasure. By the time she could think again, she had already realised that she didn't care why the sexy twin was there or whether he saw her – it aroused her to know that he was watching. She arched up into Daniel's mouth as he did something magical with her clit, then she turned to meet the twin's eyes again and lifted her hands to her breasts, caressing her own body as he watched.

She held his hungry gaze for a long minute, but his eyes finally travelled down her body and she imagined that he was watching her lift and caress her breasts, pinch her nipples and tease her fingers over her skin, even as she moaned and writhed from the pleasure that Daniel was expertly giving her.

The twin – Jake? – shifted his stan wated hisce, and she recognised something in the motion. He was unfastening his pants. Between the pleasure that Daniel was giving, the pleasure she was taking for herself, and this new rush of visual stimulation, Kris was overwhelmed. Her orgasm caught her by surprise, tearing through her in a rush that made her clamp her legs around Daniel's head and bite her own wrist to keep from screaming.

She panted and gasped for air as Daniel licked patient, slow strokes across her pussy while he waited for her to regain control. Each of those slow licks sent a shudder of pleasure running through her like an aftershock, and she moaned and ground herself against his tongue.

He stood, smiling, and pulled a condom from his pocket, his eyebrows raised inquisitively. Her eyes flicked to where Jake was hiding under the risers, met his hot gaze, and then flicked back to Daniel. 'Yes, I want you to fuck me,' she said. He was out of his pants in record time, and she sat up and took the condom away from him, sliding it onto his hot length herself.

He started to push her gently back, but Kris shook her head and shifted, turning onto her hands and knees and looking back over her shoulder invitingly. Daniel made a sound of approval and moved up behind her, rubbing his cock through the moisture of her pussy before he shifted his angle and pressed the head of his cock against her hole. She moaned and tossed her head back, pressing into him until he slid deep inside her.

She writhed against him and he quickly took his cue, sliding back to thrust deep into her, his hands clamped tight on her hips. Kris thought for an insane second that she could fall in love with him just for knowing what she needed in that moment. But no, this was something else – passion, lust, drive – and though it was transient, it had her completely in its hold for now.

She braced her arms on the platform and pushed back into his thrusts, sending his cock slamming deep and hard inside her. He picked up his rhythm and she cried out and moved with him as their fuck became even more intense. Her pussy tingled with renewed energy and desire, and she raised one hand, her fingers moving over her clit in a dance that made her toes curl.

When Daniel lifted one hand from her hip and reached up to pinch and roughly twist her nipple, it was all Kris needed to fly. She felt as if she were swinging from a trapeze high over the ring or flying through the air, her entire body sensitised and soaring with pleasure. When she turned her head enough, she could see Jake's arm working furiously as he watched her with hungry eyes. Behind her, Daniel still thrust hard; grunting with pleasure as he continued to drive sparks through her.

'Wait,' she said, and he immediately stopped, though his breath came in heavy pants. She moved forward and he slid out of her with a moan and a wet sound, and she stepped into the ring and pulled him with her. 'Sit,' she said, and he obediently sat on the platform. She turned her back to him and lowered herself down, and he held his cock at the perfect angle to slide right into her.

She closed her eyes and focused on the sensation of being filled as she lowered herself all the way down. Then she tensed her legs and his hands on her waist helped her form a quick rhythm. The angle of his cock seemed to tease at her sensitive flesh and she moaned and let her hands wander, one teasing between his balls and her own clit, the other reaching up to caress her breasts and toy with her nipples.

She locked her eyes on Jake, and the thought of what his hand was doing as he furiously pumped his arm only added fuel to the erotic fire as Daniel's cock slid in and out of her, filling and stretching and arousing her. Though it made her cheeks flush with embarrasll ith embsment, she couldn't help but picture Jake coming forward to tease her body with his strong hands or place his cock in her mouth. She'd never been with two men at once, and she wasn't even sure she wanted to, but the images in her mind made her wild with arousal.

Jake licked his lips as he watched her, and she winked at him as she clamped a hand down on her breast and squeezed hard. She was so close she could taste it, and from behind her, Daniel's moans were getting intense. Then she shifted her hips slightly, and the pleasure was like nothing she had ever experienced.

Suddenly the angle of Daniel's cock drove into something deep and incredible inside her, and she let out a long, low moan of pleasure as the level of stimulation swept past what she thought she could endure and her entire body seemed to clench in one massive, full-body orgasm, liquid gushing from her body like a broken dam. Daniel let out a long groan of pleasure, keeping them both moving as he joined her in pleasure. Through a red haze of ecstasy she watched Jake's face contort in his own private pleasure, then she dropped her head back onto Daniel's shoulder, limp and exhausted.

Daniel chuckled breathlessly as he reached around to run his fingers through the product of her arousal. He brought his fingers to his lips and made an appreciative sound. 'Damn, girl, you are one wild lady.'

'You have no idea.' She looked up, but Jake was already gone. 'I think I need to lie down.' Daniel chuckled and helped her onto the platform. He got his clothes on first, then came back and helped her dress like some big doll or a helpless child, although when she tried to be useful she did have a hard time breaking through the aroused languor.

'Morning comes early here. Best if I take you home,' he said, and once her shoes were in place, he helped pull her to her feet. She wrapped an arm around him and took deep breaths until she was able to keep her feet under her, though each step sent a tingling jolt through her clit. Outside the tent, Jake was still loitering. 'Oh, hey Josh. Jake was looking for you earlier,' Daniel said.

'I'll go find him,' Josh said. He winked at Kris and licked his lips as she went past.

'Josh?'

'Sure. They were wearing different shirts. You learn to watch for those things or you'd never be able to tell them apart.'

It was the other twin? Kris laughed as she climbed up into Daniel's old truck.

Cabaret Girls
Olivia London

I was the new girl in town. Sashaying down the street wearing just enough skirt not to get arrested, I was a walking target for adventure. I found just what I was looking for with Bella, the best-looking chick at PJ's Cabaret on Broadway. Bella went on stage occasionally, belting out songs the way a venal middleweight delivers punches. Maybe she could have been a contender but there was something elliptical, something defensive in her voice that put audiences off until they fulfilled the two drink minimum. It would take a long while before I found out what this buff babe did for a living. I didn't care. I wasn't looking for a girlfriend or my soul mate. Before moving to San Francisco, every day held no more excitement or an ounce more of texture than a bowl of oatmeal. I wanted nights glazed with marzipan and cherries. Life, if lived to the fullest, had to *taste* like something.

Bella tasted like hops, sugar and wine, perhaps because she lived on all three. We met in the middle olivf the night, our bodies calling out to each other like island castoffs looking to be saved. There was a Casual Dating column in a free weekly paper. Back in the day, a 'casual date' was code for strangers who wanted to hook up, fuck each other's brains out and skedaddle. Animal sex. Raw rogering. The kind of coupling that was only good with a stranger you knew would remain a stranger like a masked mystery at a costume ball.

My date paid for the room. I was too busy checking her out to notice the overpowering smell of chemicals drifting from the hot tub. I laid some towels down on the canvas pad countless people had used as a makeshift bed, presumably for illicit purposes. It was no secret that hookers and their johns took advantage of places like this.

'How do you want it?' the stranger asked, smirking knowingly.

'Whatever you can give me, I want *now*,' I said, matching her attitude if not upping the ante. 'That's why I'm here. I just want to get off.'

Bella's black spiky mane appeared shiny even under dim lights. Her hair seemed as much armor as the torn black leather jacket she quickly tossed to the side, knocking over a bowl of complimentary breath mints.

'Take off your skirt and bend over my lap,' she commanded.

I thought she'd fingerfuck me from behind or tickle

18

my crack with a butt plug, but no. From the first slam of her palm on my goose bumped flesh, I knew I was in for a sound spanking.

Her slaps came down evenly and succinctly until I squirmed, accidentally scratching the skin beneath her cargo pants.

She pulled me up by the hair, surprising me with a kiss, her tongue probing so sweetly, I shuddered with delight.

'You need to trim those fingernails, hon,' she said gently.

Then, it was back to a no-nonsense paddling. Her hands were an ode to rhythm; unlike her voice, her palms were born to perform. The cadence of smacks could not be measured against the pleasure she gave. I could feel my bum burning with sensation and wanted only to be branded with her version of love. She was all over me now and my pelvis bucked, welcoming the chaos of her swats.

Finally, she turned me over, straddling my torso.

'That's what I think of femmes who just want to get off,' she whispered while running her tongue along my temple.

I lifted the T-shirt she was wearing and was amazed to see she had bound her bosom in gauze. At first I had just assumed she was flat-chested.

'Why do you do this?' I asked, too curious to worry about my stinging behind. 'Breasts are beautiful.'

Bella snorted. 'On you, doll. What? Are you turned off now?'

'Just the opposite. Touch me and see how turned on I am.'

She let one sinewy arm snake between my legs. I smiled at her reaction.

'You hot chick. Where have you been all my life?'

'Tell you later. Information traded only on satisfaction.'

Bella worked my clit with her finger pads, massaging the pip until it ached with a need to be sucked. When she plunged her digits into my vulva, I cried out shamelessly begging for more.

'Fuck me,' I begged. 'Don't stop.'

She didn't stop. She plugged my pussy with her fingers, packing my vagina with as much passion as it could hold. Having brought me to orgasm that way, she quickly tugged off her pants and mounted my glistening mound.

Our pussies were meant for each other. Her clit snicked into place over my nub while she rode my labia with her own. While our mounds locked in a fevered embrace, Bella's mouth covered mine as we fucked and sucked each other's tongues like we were the very first people to discover sex. Sex with one's own sex. So free. So uninhibited.

I wished it would last forever, or at least all night.

But this wasn't that kind of date.

We were kissing and lathering each other's bodies in the shower when a voice over an intercom told us we had ten minutes to wrap up, take our business elsewhere. Chop, chop.

It was a little unnerving but … what did I expect?

I knew how guys responded to the question: When will I see you again? I couldn't risk Bella rolling her eyes at me or worse, speaking words that sounded sincere only to prove false.

We walked outside into a mild September breeze. I was instantly glad I had parked my ride at the far end of the lot.

'I'll walk you to your car,' she offered.

I gulped, feeling far more naked than I was twenty minutes earlier. I pointed to a teal blue number that had cost me less than a week's pay; it was the vehicular equivalent of a paper weight. 'Actually, that's me over there. The scooter.'

Bella guffawed. 'A baby bike! That's so precious. I wish I could tuck you in my back pocket and take you home.'

I wish you could, too, I thought. Home for me was an apartment in North Beach without even a cat for company.

'Look,' she said, leveling her gaze to meet the query in my eyes. 'I'm embroiled in a sticky situation right now. We made a connection and I really like you. Give me your number and I'll call when I'm not so … complicated.'

I shrugged. It was a ridiculous ritual but one that begged to be gotten through. I wrote my info on a cocktail napkin and watched Bella hop on her motorcycle. She drove a Yamaha Route 66: a real bike.

I watched her pull away knowing I'd never see her again. Still, I didn't regret meeting Ms. Sex on Wheels. That was the most excitement I'd ever had in my life. The next time I masturbated, I would simply close my eyes and think of Bella. She tried to look tough but her heart-shaped face, soft hands and delicate mouth betrayed how beautiful she really was.

And the way she kissed and caressed my bottom after the spanking proved she was a giver not just a taker. If only she had looked over her shoulder as she pulled out of the parking lot; I would have followed her to the moon if she had dared me.

* * *

In the morning, I considered calling in sick but knew my voice would have sounded too elated to fool anyone. I had a dreary, albeit well-paying, job at an insurance company and I didn't dare lose it. I had moved to a *very* expensive city. My employer was a severe woman who never smiled and always wore pantsuits with those embarrassing frilly shells that went out of style in the 70s. She caught me daydreaming twice and pulled me into her office.

'You're having difficulty concentrating today, Ashley. Is there a problem?'

'No, Ma'am.' And then, because her lips made no effort to move and she wasn't going to dismiss me without further explanation, I added, 'I met someone.'

'Indeed.' Steepling her branchlike fingers, she sat up straight in her leather wingback chair. 'If In sair. catch you dawdling again I'll require you to compose a memo to me explicating the exact reasons for your inability to focus. If that's not enough to rein in your imagination you'll want to have a contingency plan.'

No doubt about it: Ms. Swanson was a first-rate bitch. To this day, I can't remember her first name. It began with a 'P', I think. Once, during my first week on the job, I addressed her as something other than 'Ms. Swanson'. She pulled me aside and said, 'Ashley, in this office, superiors will be addressed by their surnames.'

The faux pas was reflected in a fun house mirror of other transgressions I'd make until finally mastering a labyrinth of office etiquette rules.

Of course this superior was the object of relentless fantasies. She wasn't a woman I wanted to have sex with but she loomed large in an imagination that would not be quashed.

If Ms. Swanson knew how I climaxed to images of her working as a spandex-clad dominatrix, spanking bosomy secretaries prone to coffee spills and typos, she would have sent me manacled and defeated to Alcatraz for sure.

Funny how movies filmed in San Francisco never focus on the working class. All the shots would have to be black and white and everyone would look the same because working stiffs all shop at the same thrift stores. Since I didn't come from a rich family, I had to experience glamour obliquely. Let my body be my passport.

***

When Bella surprised me with a phone call, I was more than ready for another adventure.

'Hi, hot chick,' she said, by way of greeting. 'You forgot to tell me where you've been all my life.'

'Ha. I moved here from Florida. Had to work a lot of jobs before I could save up to come here, the Promised Land.' Florida! For all the sweet manna in heaven I would never go back to that state. I keep hoping the bugs will carry it off so the alligators can cavort without the constant threat of human malice.

'Hmm. Well, I'm calling to invite you to a party tomorrow. In fact, let's make a day of it. I'll take you to lunch, we'll do a little sightseeing and then it's off to Twin Peaks for a good time in the hills. Sound doable?'

I scratched my chin. 'As luck would have it, I'm only working in the morning tomorrow. Our office is shutting down for some asbestos cleaning. Only … I don't have any Kim Novak outfits to wear to a gala in the Peaks.'

24

'You really are a femme! We'll go shopping tomorrow. Ashley, hon, I'm going to show you the real San Francisco and you're going to like it very much.'

I had no doubt about that.

* * *

First we went to Fisherman's Wharf for some whiskey crab soup. Next stop: Ghirardelli Square to gorge on hot-fudge sundaes.

There was a boutique that seemed custom-made for wayward blondes travelling with well-heeled lesbian friends on their way to a party in the hills. Bella picked out and purchased a pair of Capri pants along with an embroidered madras shirt.

'Voilà!' my new friend said, handing over the glossy embossed bags. 'Instant, appropriate, soirée attire.'

When Bella took me by the hand and dragged me into the Wax Museum, I said, 'You've got to be kidding.'

'C'mon. It'll be fun. It's probably deserted on a weekday.'

'All the more reason not to be trapped >Fi be train the Chamber of Horrors.'

Who would have thought a wax museum would be the best place in the city to make out? As I shuddered at the *Titanic* display, Bella slipped her warm palms under my shirt and cupped my breasts, grazing each nipple with her thumbs.

25

We didn't last long in the Bloody Chamber. Every time I shrieked, she covered my mouth with her sensual lips. After making out in every room, we left the dark strange world for the promise held by the rest of the day.

'You left your bike at home,' I said, stating the obvious when she opened her car door for me. A shiny new BMW.

'What do you do for a living, Bella?'

She checked her rearview mirror before backing out into traffic. 'I'm a bartender.'

'No, seriously.'

Giving me a sideways glance, she said, 'Seriously. This car was a gift from my aunt.'

OK. So I was on my way to a bash with a woman who trussed her boobs and was possibly mafia connected. Welcome to my world.

***

An elegant woman wearing a white silk tank over perfectly tan skin answered the door. She ushered us past the tiled foyer into the main living room where women were huddled in pairs and groups. I was instantly aroused before checking my naughty thoughts at the door. Bella could unspool the very threads off my back, leaving me naked and hitching a ride if I so much as ogled another woman's décolletage.

Was she the jealous type? I had no idea. Much as I

had enjoyed our day, I still didn't know this woman who held me in such carnal thrall.

A margarita was placed in my hand and then another. Someone had told Mira, the hostess, margaritas were my downfall. I tried to figure what kind of soirée this was even as the tequila coated my palate and curled my tongue most pleasantly.

I was led to an outdoor patio where several women were entwined in a sunken L-shaped pool. The view of the San Bruno Mountains couldn't compete with so much exposed womanly flesh. The pool's water was crystal clear. I could see hands touching genitals. One woman with bright-red hair arched her back and played with her own vagina.

Mira produced a scarf from a pocket of her linen shorts. She bent down and blindfolded the contorted woman.

'Now, someone be nice and play with Tina.'

Mira looked from me to Bella expectantly, but we stood frozen in place. The golden-haired goddess shrugged and took off her clothes. She had no tan lines and I could just see her spending day after idle day frolicking at nude beaches.

The woman named Tina was lifted by her underarms out of the pool. Still wearing the blindfold, she gasped with pleasure as Mira's face disappeared between her inner thighs.

I couldn't believe what I was seeing. I had heard of live sex shows but assumed they were relegated to sleazy men's clubs and the sex industry's equivalent of the vaudeville circuit. Bella relaxed her hand on my shoulder as if we were casually watching fireworks.

Two others joined the scene. They had been drinking in the living room but were now both naked. A petite woman with sleek, long black hair curled like a shrimp into the supine love interest now cresting toward orgasm. A short, muscular blonde took the other side, bookending the blindfolded woman as they tweaked her nipples and caressed her belly.

It was too much. I grabbed Bella's hand and told her I wanted to go hod, ted to me. No sooner had I shut the car door though, I realised my panties were as wet as if they'd been dropped into the pool.

Without giving her a chance to resist, I yanked Bella's arm to my crotch.

'You need to get me off, right now. You got me into this mess.'

With one pull, my date torqued my panties round her fist. I leaned into the driver's side and let her fuck me with her fingers. My loins were shaking; I wanted to get fucked so badly. She tilted my torso to achieve better purchase and soon I was coming on her hands, grabbing her shoulders and crying with relief.

We drove home in silence but she continually reached

over and stroked my hair and brow. I desperately wanted to know what she really did for a living but a part of me didn't want any more knowledge for a while. I looked out the window and this time took in the view of the glorious mountains.

Bella dropped me off at my North Beach apartment. I politely thanked her for lunch and for the clothes. I never expected to see her again, not that I didn't want to. She was a mystery; if I could get beneath the gauze of her breast wrap, a story would surely unfold.

* * *

I ran a bath and let my body disappear beneath a cloud of bubbles. It felt so good to be in my own place with views of kitchen workers dumping garbage and Italian women hanging clothes on wooden pins.

Bella. Charming, inscrutable Bella. Why did she have to be so beautiful? To picture her was to want to be touched by her. I touched myself instead. I let my fingers glide over my belly and down to my vulva. I imagined my fingers were Bella's digits pinching and probing, pumping my pussy over and over again.

I hunched over in the bath, my vagina aching from the sensations of another come. What would it be like to share a balneal moment with the raven-haired beauty? I closed my eyes and saw Bella's face. I shook my head to clear it; I got out of the tub determined to steer clear of wild women who could lead down a crooked path. I had no sooner towelled off when the phone rang.

'Hi, Ashley. We need to talk.'

'Really? That's interesting because I don't have your phone number. You never gave it to me. It's bad enough I have a control freak for a boss. I don't know what kind of world you're *embroiled* in but it's not for me. You're a dangerous woman, Bella. Sexy, but dangerous. Goodbye.'

'I'll give you my number. First, let me ask: how long have you been in San Francisco? Two weeks? Three?'

'Two whole months,' I said, a tad defensively.

'I was born and raised here. You don't know what it's like to be a woman trying to survive in this town. You have a lot to learn.'

'Maybe you're not the one to teach me.'

'I am,' she sighed. 'My real name is Isabella. Let's start from there.'

'My name is really Ashley. Nice to meet you, Isabella.'

I pictured the heart-shaped face at the other end of the line and wondered what my next life lesson would be.

The next night I met my heart's desire at the cabaret joint where she sang some nights and bartended on others.

***

Women who had made unconventional livelihoods strutting onstage at PJ's Cabaret were milling about, their breasts bare save for glittering pasties. They were all shapes and /p> shapessizes with no discrimination toward age. They billed themselves as 'The Cabaret Girls' even though one woman was old enough to be my grandmother. That was cool. Their act though was forgettable with out-of-sync gyrations and giggles that morphed into shrieks.

The next act was a stand-up comic who was quite good until she forgot one of her own punch lines and turned belligerent on a heckler.

I was about to wonder why Bella (the name Isabella would take some getting used to) asked me to join her at PJ's when there she was, standing in front of a microphone and looking directly at me.

'This is for Ashley,' she told the nodding crowd, 'my new ladylove.'

If you've never been serenaded in front of dozens of lesbian couples and a dancing troupe wearing nothing but short shorts and pasties, well, I'm sorry for your troubles.

Bella crooned my favourite Tracy Chapman song and, though she sang it off-key, I was touched that she'd go to such lengths to woo a newbie in town with a staid job at an insurance firm. Her life was definitely more intriguing and she seemed to want to share it with me. She was a white girl trying to sound black. A tough chick who couldn't hide her softness. Drove a car no part-time bartender could afford. These contradictions that first gave pause were now driving me into her arms.

* * *

We held hands walking down Broadway. She opened the passenger door and I slid in, the contours of my body eagerly conforming to the cushiony seat. I was wearing the madras shirt and Capri pants she bought for me at Fisherman's Wharf.

I pulled her to me and kissed her. 'Why did we have to meet through an ad, Bel?'

She nuzzled my neck, tilting my chin for another kiss. 'We were both horny, that's why. But I've got a plan to get you away from that grim day job of yours. You're going to be so glad you met me … if you'll forgive my lack of modesty.'

I stroked her chest under the proverbial leather jacket she wore like a second skin and was relieved she hadn't trussed her breasts again.

There was no telling if we'd make it back to her place in Pacific Heights without crashing. The attar of new BMW upholstery filled my nostrils and admittedly elevated what might otherwise have been a tawdry experience. I was having difficulty shaking the image of all those pasties blinking at me like bike reflectors.

Bella owned a condo off Clay Street: another red flag. Before I could admire the artwork on the walls and *objets d'art* daubing every available surface, my lover was tying my wrists behind a ladder-back chair and diving between my legs. She fastened her lips to my clit and let her tongue go haywire. It was maddening not being able to touch her back. Every time she pulled away to fork her fingers into my sex I wanted to push her face back to my pussy where it belonged.

But she was a giving lover so when I begged her to fuck me with her tongue she did. She licked my lobe frantically until I was rocking in my seat. She kept my loins parted until they were trembling and she adjusted her palate to my labia as if sampling a fine liqueur.

When her lips moved in tandem with her fingers I thought I'd melt from sheer pleasure. She made me feel like the most beautiful woman in the world as she licked and loved my quim like it was the most precious thing ever.

Finally sated, she led me to her bedroom where we made exquisite love, enjoying each other with luscious abandon. She had a symbol tattooed to o ttattooeher sternum. I kissed round the familiar icon, tracing a trail down to her own sweet mound. Her pussy was tighter than a snapped reticule and lavish with nectar. She came readily enough as I fingerfucked her moist mound with only one digit and let my tongue orbit her labia till I thought I'd go dizzy with my own ministrations.

* * *

We must have set a record for orgasms. She surprised me
in the morning with coffee and scones. Above the aroma
of my favourite brew and pastries reticent of cinnamon
and butter, I could still smell and taste her female gifts.
The promise of sex permeated the air and clung to our
clothes. My ears were still ringing from shouts fisting
from under the covers. My jaw hurt. It was a good thing
I didn't have to face my boss for another two days. I
needed time to recover.

I thought it would be awkward seeing Bella in normal
light but one of her many talents was for lending normalcy
to the less intrepid. I tried not to think where this relationship was headed. Tried only to savour the moment.

'What are you thinking, Ashley?' She tucked a stray
lock over my ear.

'I'm thinking it's unusual for someone our age to have
an original Diane Arbus photograph hanging in the foyer.
I know you don't come from money.'

She leaned back in her seat and picked at her scone.
'Like I said, this town eats women alive. If you stick
with me, you'll always eat well.'

'We'll see, Bella. We'll see.'

Shining Knight
Flora Dain

'Get in.'

The limo blocks my path, the rear door already yawning open. It screeched to a halt right up on the kerb, blocking the end of the alleyway, leaving me nowhere to run.

The men behind me are gaining now, their trainers pounding the pavement. They're nearly on me, laughing to each other as they close in.

To them it's a game.

I got a head start with a sharp knee to a groin and made for the side roads but I can't run far. My skirt's too tight, my heels too high and I'm desperate.

I've no time even to kick them off.

At the first lunge of the gang towards my plunging neckline – ripping the thin satin away from one breast, exposing the upper curve of the other – they sensed fear.

My dash to escape was pure panic – a blind deer-leap for freedom at a whiff of wolf.

My one hope was the high street. It's late now, well after midnight, but surely someone will see me, look up at the chase, be startled enough or kind enough to call the police …

But now the limo bars the way and the pack's almost here.

I've no choice. I launch myself through the open door as eager hands from behind clutch at what's left of my three-thousand dollar Alaïa. I collapse into the upholstered luxury of the back seat, fighting for breath.

The car speeds away, silent and swift, and I'm safe.

Or am I?

The man sitting at the other end of the seat is elegant and unruffled. I envy him his calm.

He has clearly not just run for his life from a gang of eager young males intent on mayhem. His ankle is not twisted, his eyes are not wild and he's not clawing in great lungfuls of air, his chest straining with pain t sCand effort.

The car is enormous but he's sitting alone. His piercing gaze both strips me naked and disapproves at the same time.

His eyebrow lifts, faintly sardonic. 'Friends of yours?'

'No,' I rasp. He thinks I run about the streets just for *fun*?

I take hold of myself. This is no time to lose my temper. I owe him.

I can just about speak now but pain darts through my chest like needles. About four streets ago my lungs seemed to lose the use of oxygen. Now it's slicing back.

'Thank you for ...' I tail off.

I want to thank him for rescuing me, this shining knight who's scooped me up from an alleyway like a stray cat, but I pause, lips parted.

Is he a shining knight? Or an enemy? Maybe I've escaped one foe only to fall foul of another.

Past his shoulder I catch my reflection in the car window. Is this what he sees? My grandmother came from Naples. I owe her my full, sculpted mouth, long legs and striking figure.

My looks can cause me problems, like they did just now. My passionate nature's far worse but that's hardly her fault. That's all me.

Tonight it's brought me to this. And as I take a good look at my rescuer it's my undoing now.

He's stunningly handsome, and not just in a regular, look-at-me-I'm-rich kind of way. There's a delicate appeal in the tilt of his eyebrows, a hint of power in the set of his jaw, arrogance in the flare to his nostrils.

Irresistible.

Our eyes lock and in that instant I'm lost. I'll do whatever this man wants me to do. And from the way his eyes are feasting on my heaving breasts, scanty, torn dress and alley-spattered limbs I'll probably have to.

He frowns. 'Do you need a hospital? Police?'

He wants to know if I was attacked. I shake my head and count my blessings. 'No. I just panicked when they tore my ...' I tail off.

He can see what they tore. His eyes have barely left the spot.

I flinch as he leans forward. He hesitates, eyeing me with a flicker of concern. I sit very still as he pulls my gaping neckline down a little further to expose the other breast.

His touch is like fire, just the lightest brush of his fingers but it shimmers on my skin like electricity. An answering tremor runs all through me, straight to my groin.

'That's better. More symmetrical.' He leans back and eyes me with satisfaction, like I'm some rare ornament he's just improved by moving it a fraction to the left.

Whoa. *What's going on here?*

'I'm not a taxi service. But I'll drive you wherever you like as long as you're willing to accept ... certain terms.'

Terms? My mind races with thrilling, unspeakable possibilities.

It seems my rescue comes at a price.

'Or I can drop you off now and you can go back to your friends, or not, as you wish. Which would you like?'

His manner is friendly but his tone is sharp. His mouth sets in a firm line, leaving no room for negotiation.

'I'll stay.' My response is firm and prompt, perhaps too prompt.

A flicker of satisfaction crosses his face and then is gone. Maybe I dreamed it.

'OK, your call. Come closer.' His voice is low, his steady gaze giving nothing away.

Slowly, unsure what I think about this, I edge towards him along the seat. He watches me with a gleam, the intensity of his look sending tremors of excitement all through me, making the down rise all along my arms, making my nipples stiffen and swell.

He sees them. He says nothing, but a faint twitch at the corner of his long mouth warns me he's taken them into account. He eyes them appreciatively, a low murmur somewhere deep in his throat.

The sound of it stirs something in me too. Deep down I begin to pulse.

'Delightful. Now I want you to offer them.'

I stare at him in dismay. It occurs to me that I've accepted his terms but I forgot to ask what they were.

Too late now. I must play this by ear.

The gleam in his eyes is my only guide to his feelings as I cradle my breasts in my hands and fondle them suggestively, making them bulge and swell.

Is this what he wants?

'Offer them like you mean it.' His voice lowers to a breathy purr and I press harder, pushing out my nipples with my fingers and thumbs, rolling them slightly and giving them a hard pinch or two to make them rosy.

His breathing quickens, his lips part. *'Press back your shoulders.'*

I do as he asks, arching my back so I can thrust them forward.

I have firm, generous breasts – another Neapolitan legacy. And a get-out-of-jail card.

Why is this so hot? This simple act of submissive display is burning me up.

He dips his head to touch his lips first to one and then to the other, sucking in a great mouthful of each, nipping and tormenting my nipples with his teeth.

I throw back my head and groan as his hot, eager mouth sets me on fire.

He straightens up with a faint smile, eyes agleam, and leans back on the seat.

It's a greeting of sorts but it hardly prepares me for his next move.

Without any warning he seizes me by the waist and hauls me over his lap. He pushes me down headfirst towards the floor and grabs one of my legs, ducking his head underneath so my knees are at either side of him and my elbows are leaning on the floor.

'What are you doing?' Shock makes me shrill, shame

40

makes me crimson. The car's windows are blank from outside but from where I'm looking motorists are leering in at the darkened windows, rubber-necking for celebs.

Naturally they can't really see me but that's not what it feels like.

He pushes me down further and now my head's down low, my ass high up. My forehead presses into the carpet. It's soft and faintly perfumed. His valeting service, like everything else about him, must be very expensive.

'What do you think I'm doing?' His voice is calm and low, his grip surprisingly strong. My arched feet are way up on the seat at either side of his head, my cleft spread wide and fully displayed as I try to twist over.

'Keep still.' He delivers a hard, stinging slap on my bottom and I shriek. Instantly his hands caress my naked, exposed rear while my most private places yawn wide across his thighs like an open book.

'No panties? No wonder you were followed. You deserve a thoroughly sound –' he slaps me again, and once more I yell 'His m lell ' spanking. So I'd better give you one.'

'What? You can't do this,' I gasp. 'Not here.'

'Well guess what, I just did. And now I'm doing it again.' He slaps me a few times more and then pauses. One hand slips casually into the wide gap splayed over his knees.

41

'And what have we here? Someone's wet. How interesting. Let's see how much wetter we can make you.'

He's stroking me now, his hands kneading my rump like it's dough. His hands ... his touch is firm, warm, provoking. It's sort of like a massage except I can't relax. I'm getting more rigid by the second at the thought of what's coming.

'What were you running away from?'

I flush and squirm. I've no answer to this. 'It seemed a good idea at the time,' I mutter.

He slaps me again, a mere taster, I'm sure, but I gasp at the sting of it.

'Was that wise, exposing yourself in the streets at this hour? You deserve this. You might have met far worse if I hadn't seen you. What were you thinking?'

I press my lips together. In truth I've only myself to blame.

'You need a lesson. And stop struggling or we'll start over.'

I writhe in protest but it's useless. I'm firmly gripped as one Gucci loafer and then the other land on my shoulder blades and pin me into position and without warning he starts, the blows coming fast and hard.

He uses now one hand, now the other. Soon I'm gasping to his rhythm, first clenching my teeth, then opening my mouth to haul in air. Arousal pounds through me, my exposed, jolting slit growing numb with *hunger, my labia swelling with need, desperate for some touch, any touch, to fire my climax as juices pool uselessly in the soft, pulsing dip between my legs that burns for bulk, craves invasion.*

'What about your driver?' I say, wildly.

He laughs softly as he strokes me again, his touch once more lulling me into contented submission, luring me to relax. 'You want him too? My, we are feeling frisky. Sadly he's busy. But I'm sure he'll be happy to oblige later.'

Down here I'm panting, my breaths noisy and ragged, but from somewhere way overhead he sounds calm, urbane. His breathing – despite the hard, pounding exercise he's giving his arms – is barely audible. He might be discussing fine porcelain.

I writhe again as a few sharp blows land right on my sweet spot, just at the top of my thighs, and for one brief, glorious moment I feel his thumbs enter me.

I pulse again. Then the blows continue.

He wants a threesome? I shudder. 'No. I mean – surely he'll hear?'

What am I saying? At this rate half the town will hear.

He feels me again and flames shoot through me.

'Possibly. So you'd better keep –' he pauses to massage me lovingly, his hands cool now on my scorching, punished backside, and then he slaps me again, hard '– very quiet.'

At last it's done and he releases me. I tumble forwards

onto the floor in a messy, flustered heap and glare back at him over my shoulder, fired up and resentful.

He eyes me coldly and unfastens his flies. 'Come here.'

Naturally I had expected this but somehow I'm surprised I want it so much. His erection springson tion sp free, looming towards me, hot, purplish and eager.

'Take it in your mouth.'

I crawl towards him and get into position, leaning over him a little to stretch my throat. He tastes wonderful; salty and rich. Heat fills my mouth as I lick him gently. I surge forwards, yawning my throat open to take him deep.

This is a really good angle. I can do this ...

He groans. 'Enough. Not to completion. I just want to feel it in your mouth.'

Disappointment plummets through me. With an effort I pull away, leaving his cock glossy and plump, slick with my saliva ... so beautiful.

This is my party piece. How could he? 'Please,' I beg. 'You're missing a real treat, I promise.'

His expression softens. 'I'm sure.' His voice drops to a purr. 'You want to finish me?'

'Yes,' I whisper. 'Very much.'

His face grows stern. 'You've behaved disgracefully. Either that or you're a doubtful character. I think you need a firm hand so I'll limit your pleasures.'

He leans back for a moment, eyeing up distances, and then issues a command. 'Now get up on the seat.'

There are long seats at the sides of the limo. They stretch all the way to the driver's cabin, which is screened off for privacy. Awkwardly I haul myself up and perch on one, out of breath and a little nervous.

This is not over, not by a long way.

He gets up and advances towards me, crouching a little to avoid the roof, his eyes alight with excitement. 'Put your arms over your head and cross them.'

Puzzled, I do so and he seizes my wrists and thrusts my hands through the looped leather straps hanging at intervals along the corner of the roof. He unhooks each one to give it a twist and I'm caught fast, my arms crossed over my head, my bottom perched on the edge of the seat, my legs spread wide.

Crouching over me he takes firm hold of my knees and pushes them wider. 'Spread your legs apart. Further.'

He's getting impatient now. He pushes my knees wide apart and pauses to survey the effect. Once again my splayed slit is open to his gaze. He seizes my ankles and pulls me further down so I'm leaning on the edge, my toes wedged against the seat opposite. Now I'm spread-eagled across the car, pinned like a butterfly.

'You're enjoying this,' I mutter through clenched teeth, as he starts to move his hands slowly all down one flank, his face close to my skin, his inspection slow, intimate, wildly arousing. 'You like to torment women in here? Is this what you do?'

'Be quiet. And keep still.' The inspection takes a while. I find it hard to hold the position but each time I move he frowns and jerks me back into place, clearly irritated.

His touch is like electricity: delicate, provoking, carefully bypassing my most sensitive places and lingering on areas I'd no idea were so responsive. Torture – or is it worship? His lips, tongue and teeth are tasting, teasing, nipping everywhere – my taut, quivering navel, my forced, straining armpits, the soft, quivering skin inside my thighs.

After his thorough spanking I'm burning hot, all fired up with nowhere to go, and now I'm shaky all over, rippling at his touch.

'What were you doing in the street? I want to know.'

'I'm not telling you.'

'No? Why not? You want to annoy me?'

Something in his tone warns me that might be unwise. But I'm rattled now. 'You're taking advantage.'

'That's no answer. You think I'm selfish? We'll see about that.'

He kneels between my legs and fastens his mouth on my sex, his tongue thrusting deep into my folds, his hands leaning on my thighs, forcing me open. He finds my hard, throbbing little centre and jabs at it with pulses of his tongue, making me writhe and gasp.

My climax has been building since the instant I saw him and now it threatens to explode, but he pulls away a little and smiles up into my face, his dark eyes liquid.

'*Is this what you want?*'

I groan. 'You know it is.' I struggle, my arms aching now, as the promised pleasure is denied once more. I can't take much more of this, but he's taking his time. He holds all the cards.

He leans down again, his lips soft and teasing on my wet, throbbing slit, and kisses me gently, murmuring low in his throat like he's tasting fine wine. 'Delicious. Essence of slut. I could drink you all night.'

With a low, appreciative growl he fastens on me again and this time his tongue and then his teeth home in, right on the spot. Within seconds I do explode, my climax crashing through me in waves. I buck and thrash under his mouth like a doe in the jaws of a leopard.

It's glorious. I hang across the car, at sea on my orgasm, floating on the gentle waves of pleasure that ripple away leaving me loose and content.

'*Now me.*'

My eyes snap open and I tense with alarm as he leans up over my body, his erection still free, even bigger now, his intention still plain, his own pleasure still unsatisfied. He flips me over, limp as a doll, and now I'm bent over the seat again, ass in the air, arms pinioned straight this time, primed for his lust.

He covers me with his body, his torso hard against my soft, contented curves, his erection a distinct statement of virile power that robs me of breath. He breathes in

47

my ear, and it prods at me gently, mocking my softened limbs, craving entry and daring me to beg.

'Do you want me inside you?'

'Yes, yes. Now.' I gasp as he reaches round to my breasts, teasing and tweaking my heavy nipples, making me throb.

'How much? How much do you want it?'

This is torture. I can feel the head of his erection, hot and eager, pushing at my openings, big and ready. I know what to expect, I've already tasted and swallowed it, its length a surprise but its heat and its ridged, silky feel a revelation.

Now he hovers behind me, denying his own pleasure just to torment me.

'How can you do this?' I whimper. My excitement builds again, another climax swelling inside me, glowing in my belly like the promise of sunrise. 'How can you hold off for this long? What kind of man are you?'

He growls softly, close to my ear. 'I'm an angry man. You infuriate me. What were you doing in the streets? Why were you running?'

I catch my breath. 'You know perfectly well. You –'

I break off as he plunges inside me, his massive size all I'd hoped, his heat and his power invading me like flame. I give a long, happy sigh but he pulls away again, leaving me bereft, my opening empty and cold. I tremble with frustration and close my eyes, waiting, but still he holds back.

Thrill Seekers

'You wanted a thrill? You wanted strangeadynted st men all over you? Is that what you like?'

I hesitate. I'm impetuous. But why?

'Well?' He shouts in my ear, making me jump. This really matters to him.

Don't hesitate. Bad call. 'No.' I writhe in his grasp, trying to see his face, to plead with my eyes.

'You're not going anywhere. Not till you tell me.'

'I was excited. I –' I take a deep breath. 'I overreacted.'

His hand moves slowly along the underside of my belly to fasten lovingly over the wide, dripping gap waiting, quivering with need, between my legs. I hold still as his fingers splay out, easing into – everywhere.

'OK, I can accept that.'

I breathe out slowly, weak with relief that he's stopped asking me questions. I have no easy answers.

'Now you're going to apologise, and if you do it nicely maybe I'll give you what you want.' He slides his fingers into me, first two, and then three, and then maybe more – I lose count. He moves them in and out, in and out, while his erection, hotter than ever, beats a tattoo at the inner tops of my thighs, as impatient as me.

I'm starting to throb now, my private inner folds swelling with excitement, all the sensitive layers of my womanhood tingling almost to numbness with hunger for him, aching for relief, burning for his entry.

He knows this. I can feel his lips close to my ear,

stretched in a smile as he murmurs soft, sardonic crudities, aimed at inflaming me even further but I'm so hungry for him I can hardly make out the words.

'Apologise?' I manage, feebly. What does he want me to say?

He eases his tormenting hand away from my slit and holds it in front of my face. His fingers drip with my juices.

They smell earthy and real. They smell of me.

'Lick my fingers clean.'

His voice is harsh. For an instant the power is switched on and I glimpse a flash of the ruthless streak that made his millions.

Like thousands before me I blink.

I lick.

'Good girl.'

And at long last he plunges inside me. I haul at the straps, swaying slightly as the car hums softly around us. Inside me a universe of pleasure erupts as he thrusts over and over, filling me up, the soft designer fabrics of his clothes harsh on my punished bottom, his body hard and unrelenting through his shirt as he leans along my back.

Finally he pauses, his breath ragged now, his heat glowing in my belly. He reaches deep between my legs for one final, merciful caress just as he's about to come. I explode round his hand as he erupts into me, pumping and bucking his essence until I am flooded, filled and replete.

He releases me and we lie back along the seat. His arm folds around me and I lean my head on his chest. The car's slowing to a halt now. We've reached the end of our journey.

He tilts up my chin. His lips find mine in a long, lingering kiss, his tongue filling my mouth – another invasion. This time it's soft and warm and fills me with hope.

As he pulls away he takes a small box from his pocket and flips open the lid. 'This is for you.'

It's a stunning diamond ring. I look up at him aghast.

I've had a long, emotional evening, high on adrenaline. Now I'm beginning to react. My lgh react.egs tremble. Tears prick behind my eyes. 'I can't accept this. I don't deserve this.'

'I'll be the judge of that.'

He leans forward and draws a finger along my cheek. A single tear has spilled over and begins to trickle down. He wipes it away and smiles at me for the first time, a full-on, movie star smile, showing white, regular teeth.

I open my mouth to argue but his deep murmur muffles my protest like velvet.

'I planned to do this earlier. You left before I got the chance.'

He's right, I did. I left in a temper and got lost in the streets.

Passion can fire romance but it can also threaten it. Tonight I've done both but he understands. He craves my fire, he wraps me with love and he fills me with peace.

The tears are flowing freely now.

He slips the ring quietly into place on the fourth finger of my left hand and raises it to his lips, eyeing me sternly. 'And next time you walk out on me, at least have the good sense to bring enough money for a taxi.'

He kisses my fingers, his lips unbearably tender, his look searing hot.

My shining knight.

FHAFH
Elizabeth Coldwell

Rob sends the text just as Maxine and I are making ourselves comfortable in a corner booth. 'FHAFH'. I've been half-expecting it, but it still brings the heat rising to my cheeks, and sets a pulse beating hard between my legs. Our own private little code, meaningless to anyone else, but one that means this will be more than just a straightforward girls' night out. A simple acronym for a simple instruction. 'Find Him And Fuck Him'.

Maxine doesn't notice me shifting in my seat, already feeling my panties begin to dampen with a lustful flood. She's too busy trying to catch the eye of one of the waiters, shirtless, improbably muscular, and with an arch little bow tie around his neck. These topless toy boys are the main reason we come to Le Coqtail; there's nothing Maxine likes better than some young hunk fetching her drinks, so she can admire his rippled six-pack and firm ass cheeks as he bends to hand her another Long Island Iced Tea. Me, I find this display of wall-to-wall man candy a little obvious. I like my men rougher around the edges, not waxed and plucked and fake-tanned to within an inch of their life, but it was Maxine's turn to pick tonight's venue, and she had no idea my husband would be charging me with the task of finding a stranger and having sex with him before I leave here.

I mean, how can you tell a friend, even one you've known as long and trust as much as Maxine, that your husband likes you to seduce random guys, then go home and tell him every last detail while you lie together on the bed, his cock in his hand and his tongue buried in your so recently fucked pussy? No, this is something to be kept strictly between me and Rob – oh, and my man of the evening of course.

Maxine is deep in flirtatious conversation with a blond, floppy-haired waiter as I slip the phone back into my bag. Her eyes are fighting to stray higher than crotch level, which is hardly surprising. The uniform trousers here are cut to emphasise every last detail of what lurks within them, and Blondie here has plenty to show off. The satisfied little smirk on his face suggests he knows it, too.

'And my friend will have a –?' Maxine glances over at me.

I don't even nof 0eed to study the cocktail menu. 'Oh, a mojito, please.'

Blondie smirks again. Maybe it's not pride in his endowment but simply his natural facial expression. 'An excellent choice. I'll be right back with your drinks, ladies.'

The music here is loud enough that I doubt he hears Maxine exclaim, 'Did you see the size of the cock on him?' as he walks away. 'Mmm,' she continues, warming to her theme, 'what I couldn't do with something like that ...'

'Stuart away on business again, is he?' I comment dryly.

That's her cue to launch into all the details of what she's been up to – or, more accurately, hasn't been up to – since we last met up. Maxine's sex life is way more conventional than my own, and unlike me, she's happy to share all the details. Seems Stuart is overseeing some project in Luxembourg, leaving her at home with nothing but a vibrator or two for company in his absence. I'll admit to tuning out the fine details – it's not the first time Maxine's found herself in this situation, and much as I love her, I know where this story's heading and just how long it will take to get there. I'd rather spend the time discreetly scoping the room, looking out for my FHAFH, as I can't help but think of him.

The pickings are thin tonight; Le Coqtail is populated mostly by groups of women in their thirties and up, gossiping and cackling and leering over the semi-clad waiters. MILF Central, Rob always calls this place, and

I've never been sure he means it as a compliment. So I can't help wondering why he's chosen tonight to send me out on the prowl. Though not receiving any advance warning is part of the challenge. It means I haven't dressed with seduction in mind; no tiny skirt or exposed cleavage to lure my prey. Instead, I'm going to have to use my wits, my words, my natural charm, finding a man who responds to verbal cues, rather than visual. Though my nipples have been poking through my silky, pink top since I got Rob's text; forced into tense peaks by desire and anticipation. I want this, I need this, and Rob knows it. He must need it, too; it's been a while, after all.

Blondie returns with our drinks on a tray, interrupting Maxine's monologue. He sets little scallop-edged paper mats before each of us and places down Maxine's Long Island Iced Tea and my mojito down with a practised flourish. 'And here's a little something for you to try,' he adds. 'Duxelles of wild mushrooms on sourdough toast.'

The dish of little canapés, different with every round of drinks, is all part of the service at Le Coqtail, and Maxine pounces on the food with relish. 'Mmm,' she says, licking her fingers clean, 'you've got to try these, Sonia.'

I reach out and take one, popping it into my mouth. The mushroom flavour is savoury, intense, and just as delicious as Maxine suggested, but I'm distracted by the sight of the man leaning on the bar. Not having noticed him arrive, I now can't do anything but stare, drinking in the sight of his long, lean body, clad in a battered leather jacket and faded blue jeans. The outfit should be a cliché, some retro biker wannabe posing for attention, but on him it seems natural. If he has a bike parked at the kerb outside, it'll be something old but well cared for; a vintage Harley or a Triumph Bonneville, perhaps. He's drinking Mexican imported beer, straight from the bottle, and my gaze is drawn to the sight of his full lips wrapped around the neck, and the little convulsive movements of his Adam's apple as he swallows.

I don't think Maxine's noticed my attention is elsewhere; she's still grousing about how Stuart neglects her, though the diamond band sparkling on her middle finger is a present fron a preseom his last business trip to Amsterdam, and if that's neglect I know a lot of women who'd put up with it.

Now I've seen my target, I need to act fast. The guy doesn't strike me as the typical cocky young MILF-hunter who haunts this place, but he's hot and apparently unattached, and if I don't approach him, someone will.

'Max, I need the ladies'. You'll be able to amuse yourself for a while?' It's a silly question. Maxine's eyes are already alighting on our blond waiter, who's passing between the tables, looking for anyone in need of service.

Her hand rises in the air, in a beckoning gesture, and he strides towards our booth. 'I'll be fine, darling. You go powder your nose. I'm going to ask our friend here if he can explain to me the difference between shaking a Martini and stirring it …'

'OK, order me another mojito while you're at it, would you?'

I make my way in the direction of the bar, glancing back to see whether Maxine is paying me any attention. Gratified to see her head pressed close to Blondie's as she points out some item on the menu, I sidle up behind the man in the biker jacket.

Clearing my throat, I can't help but wonder what Rob is doing right now. His cock will be hard and full, I know that; he'll have been almost painfully erect since he first decided to send me out looking for a lover. But he won't be wanking, however badly he might need to come; he saves that till we're together, tormenting himself with urgent, jealous thoughts of who I might be with, and what he's doing to me. My darling cuckold; sending me out to play so he can reap the rewards on my return.

Thinking of Rob sends another pulse of lust through me. I need to make this stranger mine, for my husband's benefit. I don't bother with anything in the way of studied pick-up lines. All I need to do is make sure he notices me. 'Hi there.'

At the sound of my voice, he turns to face me. The first thing I notice is the scar running the length of his right cheek, the second eyes of a hard, brilliant blue. In combination, they give him a cruel but compelling aspect. If I wasn't so happy with Rob, so secure in the love he has for me, and his willingness to let me act out these extra-marital adventures, I'd be seriously thinking about making this more than a one-night stand. I'd want to know the story behind that scar, and the path that's brought him here, drinking by himself in a gaudy, over-priced cocktail bar. A quick glance at his left hand, the hand holding his beer bottle, shows no wedding band and no telltale pale ring of flesh to indicate he's only playing at being single.

'Hi.' He smiles a broad, white smile, and my pussy floods again. 'You've managed to escape from your friend, I notice.'

'You've been watching me.' It's not an accusation; quite the opposite.

'I might have looked over once or twice.' He drains the last of his beer, sets the empty bottle down on the bar counter. 'Can I get you a drink?'

I shake my head. 'Thanks, but I came over here with a proposition for you. I was sent out on a mission tonight.'

'Really?' His look is sceptical, assessing. Has someone played twisted little mind games with him in the past?

'Yeah, by my husband.' He makes to turn away, sure now that I'm messing with him, but I catch him by the arm, and lower my voice, not wanting to be overheard. 'My mission was to come out tonight, get fucked, then go home and tell him all about it.'

'Are you serious?' All his attention is on me n hin is onow.

'Absolutely. And you're the man I want to tell him about. What do you say?' When he hesitates, I tell him, 'This is a once-only offer, and I need an answer now, before my friend stops trying to get into that waiter's pants for a minute and sees me talking to you.'

'She's not in on this?'

'Hasn't got a clue.'

'So what's the catch?' He's had more than one opportunity to turn me down now, and still he just looks at me, those so-blue eyes almost burning through my top to the minimal bra beneath.

'There is no catch. I just want you to fuck me, right here, right now.'

He runs his tongue slowly over his bottom lip, as though considering my proposition, and for a moment I'm convinced he's going to turn me down. I've never failed in a mission before, and if he says no, I'll have to start looking for an alternative target. The thought doesn't appeal.

'OK,' he says at length. 'Let's do this. Where do you want me?'

'Well, the toilets are the traditional place,' I reply, even though the one thing I really dislike is fucking in a public toilet. Too cramped, too unsanitary however clean the facilities appear to be, and it seems rude to hog a cubicle when you know how many people might be queuing outside. More importantly, it means the stories of my adventures are gradually merging into one when I recall them. But there's no chance of me going anywhere else with my new friend; I can't leave Maxine on her own without any explanation. I can't tell her where I'm going, and who with, without revealing the truth of my arrangement with Rob. And I certainly can't leave that poor waiter, over-endowed everywhere but between the ears, in her excited clutches.

He must sense my lack of enthusiasm for the prospect, because he announces, 'I've got a better idea. Come with me.' Taking me by the hand, his grip warm and assured enough to set me tingling, he leads me round behind the bar.

'Are we allowed to do this?' I ask, though the barman doesn't bat an eyelid as my new friend takes me through an unmarked door and down a corridor where boxes containing bottles of assorted spirits and mixers are stacked high.

'My brother owns this place. He won't mind.' It's more information than I need, strictly speaking, but it's nice to know we're not breaking any rules – apart from the one that says a married woman really shouldn't have sex with a man she only met five minutes earlier, of course.

He pushes open a fire door, the metal bar swinging downwards with a loud, echoing clang. We find ourselves in the narrow alley behind the bar, deserted apart from the large metal dumpster belonging to the Chinese restaurant next door. Somewhere in the distance, a police car speeds down the street, blaring its ululating siren call. This is hardly the most glamorous environment for a quickie, but that only adds to the illicit nature of what we're about to do. And for once I won't have to tell Rob about having the scent of pine disinfectant in my nostrils as I get fucked.

The night air is cool after the overheated interior of Le Coqtail, but the goose bumps on my skin are from desire as much as the chill.

My lover pulls me into a clinch, pressing me up against the wall. His breath is hot against my neck as he murmurs, 'One thing before we go any further. Tell me your name, so I'll know whose pussy my cock is buried in.'

His words have such a powerful erotic charge I don't even consider lying to him. My fingers trace the scar on his cheek. 'It's ice. 'ItSonia.'

'Pleased to meet you, Sonia. I'm Mack.' It suits him; stark and a little unconventional. And Rob always prefers it when I get a man's name; it makes my lover into somebody in his eyes, as I weave the tale of my adventure afterwards.

'Well, I have one thing to ask you in return,' I tell him, as his mouth nips and nibbles at my neck. While his work-roughened hands roam the contours of my body, I fumble in the handbag that hangs by a thin strap from my left shoulder, and pull out a condom. 'Wear this for me.'

'Of course,' he replies, 'but why don't you put it on me? It's so much sexier that way.'

In Rob's ultimate fantasy, I don't bother with the condom. I go home with my pussy full of my lover's cum, and order him to lick out every last drop. He tells me he gets such a thrill from that humiliating thought, but he's sensible enough to know that, in real life, I need to play it safe. Though some people may argue there's nothing too safe about letting myself be fucked in an alley by a virtual stranger.

I slither down Mack's body, while he shrugs off his jacket and lets it drop to the floor. His belt buckle is heavy and ornate, and it takes me a while to wrench it open, but he just stands patiently, letting me work. My fingers brush over the bulge in his jeans; I doubt he's as big as Blondie, but what I can feel is thick and solid, ready to be unleashed.

My battle with his belt finally won, I yank down his zip. There's no underwear to impede my progress, and my fingers wrap around hot, virile cock-flesh. Even as I stroke along its length, I'm committing every detail of its heft and texture to memory. When I get home, I'll be able to tell Rob how it curved outwards from Mack's groin; how the foreskin peeled back to reveal a domed, red head, juice beading at its tip.

Bending close, I breathe in salty maleness, the scent of his cock inflaming my senses further. It's time to perform my party trick; one I've spent many hours perfecting. Ripping open the foil, I pop the condom into my mouth, tasting the flavours of mint and rubber. One hand grips the base of Mack's cock, holding it steady while I bob my head and painstakingly roll the condom in gulping movements over the head and down the shaft.

When I look back up, every last inch securely sheathed in latex, it's to meet Mack's astonished gaze. 'Wow!' he exclaims. 'I thought only hookers could do that.'

I grin. 'What, you've never had a nice girl let her inner hooker loose on you before?'

Shaking his head in wonderment, he replies, 'Your husband must be a very lucky man.'

'You don't even know the half of it,' I assure him. It won't be long before I need to have him inside me – and I'm still all too aware of Maxine, who's bound to be wondering why it's taking me so long to complete a simple trip to the ladies' – but first it's time for a spot of exploration. After all, it's not like I'm going to get the chance again.

It's a good thing there's no one around to see us, as I pull his jeans down so they're partway to his knees. No man can look elegant with his clothing in such disarray and his bare ass on display to the world, but this isn't about elegance. It's about sex and need and surrendering to the moment.

Trailing wet kisses along the inside of his thigh, I let his sighs and hissing breaths guide me toward my target. He must have been expecting a quick knee-trembler, not the feel of soft lips engulfing his balls, sucking gently and causing him to grip hard at my tousled curls in response.

Along the alley, there's the sound of a heavy door being pushed open, and feet crunching on gravel. We freeze, expecting to be caught in the act. And just how do you explain away the fact you're crouching at a man's feet with his balls in your mouth, or that your husband asked you to do this – for your own pleasure, and his? But the thickset middle-aged Chinese man who emerges is only interested in tossing a couple of black bin bags into the dumpster before disappearing back into the restaurant, responding to the voice of someone inside with an angry shout as he does so.

'That was too close for comfort,' Mack comments, as I rise from my kneeling position.

'Yeah, but aren't you turned on by it?' I ask. 'I know I am. Just think if he'd stayed around to watch us fuck ...' As I speak, I'm wanking Mack's cock through the condom, though it hasn't lost a fraction of its unrelenting hardness despite the unexpected interruption.

'God, you're a kinky little bitch, aren't you?' Mack's tone is one of thorough approval. Anything he might have wanted to add is lost as I press my lips to his in a hungry kiss. My hands are all over his ass cheeks, squeezing them.

'Fuck me,' I order him when I break the kiss. His response is to reach up under my skirt, tugging at my knickers so hard the elastic snaps. I step out of the ruined underwear, thankful I haven't worn one of my favourite pairs tonight.

Satisfied that I'm bare and ready for him – there's no question I'm slick enough; my juices are wetting the tops of my thighs – Mack hoists me up, my back to the brick. He's strong enough to hold me in place while I guide his cock to my pussy hole, then he lets me sink down on to him.

This is the part I love describing most to Rob; that delightful instant when I'm fully impaled by another man's dick, all my senses focused on the in-and-out movement that stretches and sustains and claims me. My ankles are locked round the backs of Mack's thighs, limiting his range of movement. His thrusts are hard, jerky, pushing me so hard I'm sure the marks of the brickwork will be visible on my skin, and it's a fight not to crack my head on the wall as he increases the pace. But the pressure on my clit as his body grinds against mine is just right, and every stroke sends tiny ripples of pleasure through my belly.

'That's it,' I urge him. 'Just keep doing that, and when I get home, I'll be able to tell my husband all about how hard you made me come.'

Nothing this good can last for long, and Mack seems all too aware he's on the clock here. He gives a long, ecstatic groan, and pumps his cum into the condom in a series of short bursts. My pussy muscles clamp down hard on his deeply implanted length, and my orgasm bursts and spreads like so many fireworks inside me.

He slips from me, and starts tidying himself up as I lean against the wall, legs weak, not able to trust myself to stand unsupported just yet.

'That was incredible,' he says. I think he tosses the condom in the dumpster, but I'm too busy retrieving my ruined underwear and making myself look respectable once more to reply.

Back in the warm, bright interior of the bar, we part with an embrace. 'If you ever want me again,' Mack says, 'you know where to find me.'

My smile is enigmatic; I don't usually come back for more, but for the first time in my life, I could be tempted.

When I get back to my seat, Maxine is halfway down her second Long Island Iced Tea, and my fresh mojito is nowhere to be seen. In all the excitement of flirting with Blondie, she moregetie, she than likely forgot it. At least she's been thoughtful enough to leave me what looks like a tiny goat's cheese and onion tartlet to nibble on.

'Was there a queue?' is all she asks as I plonk myself down beside her. If she notices my slightly dishevelled appearance, she doesn't point it out.

I make a non-committal reply as I reach for my drink, the taste of Mack's kisses so sweet in my mouth I'm almost reluctant to wash it away.

'You know,' she continues, 'while you were in the ladies' I was having the naughtiest thoughts about that cute blond waiter. He really does have the hugest cock. Anyway, I started thinking how much fun it might be to drag him off into a dark corner and fuck him while you sat here and waited for me to return. But of course, no one would really do anything like that, would they, darling?'

'Of course not, Max,' I reply, as I reach for my phone. 'What a ridiculous idea.'

I know the message I send to Rob will have him anticipating my return, cock harder than ever as he waits for me to come home and regale him with the juicy details. 'FHAFH'. Found Him And Fucked Him.

But Rob's going to have to wait just a little longer before he finds out who 'he' was, and how much I enjoyed my encounter in the alley. It'll add to his frustration, of course, but that's all part of the game. Beckoning the waiter over, I order another round of cocktails.

Cerise Calls It 'Research'
Giselle Renarde

Book-learnin', her grandmother called it. Cerise called it education. Nowhere near as important as street smarts.

Cerise liked to think she possessed book-learnin' and street smarts. With one degree under her belt and a graduate degree in the works, the university seemed to see her potential. Her mentor, Professor MacLaren, saw it better than anyone. With his endearing brogue and sky-blue eyes, she'd fallen for him the moment they met.

Typical.

For Cerise, falling in lust with any gay man was typical. When she decided to concentrate her undergraduate efforts on Gay and Lesbian Studies, her whole family thought she was coming out. Her grandmother was bold enough to ask, 'Does this mean you're a lesbian?'

'No, no,' she'd laughed. Women didn't interest Cerise in the least.

'*You can understand why your grandmother might ask,*' *her dad had said.* '*I don't remember the last time you brought a boy home who wasn't …*'

He didn't say 'gay' but that's obviously what he meant.

'*I'm not a lesbian.*'

The family nodded, but they kept stealing glances like they might see her true rainbow colours shining through if they caught her unexpected.

It's not like she could explain the truth of the matter, certainly not to her family. Cerise realised she had a strange predilection, but it wasn't the sort of thing she would go shouting from the rooftops.

Cerise was sexually attracted to gay men.

It was a fetish. She knew that. Straight men did nothing for her. Not even bi guys. Cerise was doomed to the realm of unrequited love, because the men she fell for never returned her affection. They might like her, even love her as a friend, but never as a romantic partner. Never as a sex objed thct.

And, God, how Cerise wanted to be a gay man's sex object!

Her gay man fetish was a Catch-22: she wanted men who loved only men, but if they went for her they'd no longer fit that category, thus she wouldn't be interested. Crazy! It gave her a headache just thinking about it.

Love was an exercise in futility, for Cerise. The friends she'd confided with her fetish claimed she was never really in love with men like Professor MacLaren. It was infatuation, empty. But she felt everything deep inside her heart. It must be real. Even if her tutor never returned her affection (and he surely never would), at least she got to see him every day.

Maybe Cerise got off on rejection as much as she got off on fantasy.

Monday morning, she went to work researching for the professor's book at eight o'clock on the dot. Not five minutes went by before she caught herself off in dreamland, imagining her sexy professor storming into her tiny office in the main library. He'd tear off her top, planting kisses down her neck and digging her swollen breasts from the lace cage of her bra. Like a beast, he'd rut between her legs, fucking her so hard she couldn't breathe, let alone scream. She'd come in silence with his hand covering her mouth, his cock pulsing in her sex.

Cerise shook her head, trying to knock those thoughts away. If she couldn't concentrate, she'd have to lock that office door and flick her clit until the ache subsided. That's how she rocked herself to sleep every night, but during the day she ought to be working. If she couldn't have Professor MacLaren all to herself, she could at least impress him with her research skills.

Her handsome gay advisor was writing a regional book about cruising in the early twentieth century. A big part of Cerise's job consisted of reviewing court documents from the 1920s. It amazed her how many cases were on record, of men arrested for sucking and fucking in public parks.

According to police records, Queen's Park was a popular spot for men who had sex with men, even a hundred years ago. Despite its proximity to campus, Cerise never walked through the park, especially not after dark. It was a wooded space, but not deeply so. If guys were fucking in there, passers-by would see them for sure. Maybe that's why so many men got caught.

Would it help with the research, Cerise wondered, if she snuck out for a brisk stroll around Queen's Park late at night? It would certainly impress the professor if she came back with information pertinent to his book. Was the park as rife with homoeroticism as it had been in the 1920s? Cerise couldn't wait to find out. Imagine if she caught a couple of guys going at it! Just the thought of a pair wedged surreptitiously between a park bench and a tree trunk, pants down, one getting ravaged while the other whispered harsh words into his ear ...

Cerise couldn't concentrate on her court documents. Imagine if she stumbled across someone she knew! Wouldn't that be wild? Especially if it happened to be one of her straight-laced tutors, or even Professor MacLaren. Sure he was out, but the guy had a husband at home. He wasn't the cruising type.

After midnight, Cerise zipped up her hoodie and

wrapped her scarf twice around her neck. It would be chilly out there in the dark. And dangerous, possibly. Good thing she carried a backpack instead of a purse. Backpacks were less likely to attract muggers.

Pulling her hood over her head, Cerise left the all-night university library. Her belly fluttered and she felt faintly like she had to pee even though she'd just gone. This was a bad idea, this 'research' she'd devised. Whatevarkised. Wer men got up to at Queen's Park, she should just leave them to it.

But a compulsion came over her, a thick pulse like a heartbeat between her legs. Her pussy led her forward.

Queen's Park was an oval of green space splitting a major city thoroughfare in two. It was bordered by the museum at the north end and the legislature at the south, with university buildings lining both sides.

Despite the many streetlamps illuminating the centre pathway, Queen's Park seemed darker than hell. Autumn leaves crunched underfoot as Cerise wrapped her scarf even tighter around her neck. The air was brisk, but that wasn't the cause of her chill. Every step she took, the ground seemed to writhe beneath her, like the very soil knew her dirty desires. This was more than just research.

There was movement to her right, and Cerise's pulse thundered in her ears. Something clenched around her heart, like the cold hand of death. Her eyes went bleary. This was the same feeling she got when she heard a good ghost story. She loved it, even if the park scared her to tears.

Cerise turned swiftly to spot a homeless man stretched out on a bench. His eyes were closed. He wasn't looking at her, but that didn't matter. Her legs were like iron, and she stared at him even though she wanted to run for the nearest subway station.

As she stood, dumbfounded, the noise of the city at night filled her ears: faraway sounds of cars and parties, people heading out while others went home. And then there were closer sounds, noises from inside the park. Faint moaning. Grunts. 'Yes, suck it. Right there.' Were they real men's voices or the ghosts of the 1920s?

Cerise tiptoed around the man on the bench, trying to slide her shoes under the leaves rather than step on them. She didn't want to make any noise. She didn't want to interrupt whatever was happening just beyond that nearby knoll.

Climbing the slight incline, Cerise crouched behind the leafless skeleton of a tall bush. The valley below was so dark. There was a streetlamp off in the distance, but the light was mostly blocked out by a group of trees. Was anybody down there? She really couldn't tell. But she couldn't move either, not until she knew for sure.

'Suck it, yeah.'

Yes! She definitely heard it that time. Where were these guys? The noises came from straight ahead. God,

*why was it so dark? Right in the middle of the city!
Cerise peered through the naked branches of her hiding
hedge, and bodies began to form. They were so nearby
she almost fell backward. The men would certainly spot
her if they stared through the bush.*

*Wait, was she sure they were men? She gazed even
more intently. Both bodies were dressed in men's clothes,
and the one standing up against a tree was much larger
than the one crouching in front of him, but those shoulders were definitely broad. Yes, they were guys. Cerise
was sure of it.*

*There wasn't a hell of a lot of motion. Other people
might saunter by without even noticing they were there.
They weren't making much noise, either. Just a soft hum
or moan here and there as the bottom gobbled the top.
His dark shoulder-length hair swayed as he bobbed at the
larger man's crotch. The scarce light from beyond the trees
shimmered like the sun on ravens' wings as those silky
strands tossed and waved. What wouldn't Cerise give to
see that boy's face? Judging by his hair, he had to be cute.*

*Cerise snuck a quick look over her shoulder to make
sure nobody was stalking her. The sleeping man still
haunted his bench, but there was no one else around. She
turned her attention back to the men beyond the knoll,
but as s shll, buthe shifted her weight her foot slipped.
Her ankle failed her. She fell to the side and her backpack brought her tumbling down through the bare bush.*

Switches slapped her cheeks as she somersaulted across the hedge, thudding down the incline. Her head jerked to the side and she winced, clawing at the grass beneath a cover of fallen leaves. She was rolling now, and she couldn't stop.

Her head smacked something. Dazed, she glanced up to see that, no, it wasn't a tree trunk. It was a leg. And it wasn't only one leg, but four. She'd somehow managed to wedge her head between the thighs of the crouching man and the shins of the standing one. When she looked straight up, she saw two stunned faces and one hard dick.

'Sorry,' Cerise stammered. 'Don't mind me.'

'What the –' The standing man buried his erection inside his pants and the kneeling man sighed.

'No, please,' Cerise begged. Her heart was racing, but it wasn't from fear. 'I mean it. Just let me … let me watch?'

The crouching man looked over his shoulders, looked all around like he expected to find a Candid Camera film crew behind him. The poor guy couldn't really move because Cerise's head was more or less resting in his lap. She didn't move, for her part, because she was so awestruck by his handsome face.

Crouchy was the kind of guy who got Cerise's gaydar and libido up. Some men were just so obviously gay. She could see it in their noses and their cheekbones. And their eyes, of course. Even if Crouchy hadn't been sporting a black jersey T-shirt with rainbow sequins on the diagonal, she'd still have known he favoured men. It was like a musk emanating from his skin, this desire for cock. He had lips that said, 'I suck dick,' even when they were pursed firmly shut.

Standy-up there was another kettle of fish. He had a square jaw and the kind of haircut that reminded Cerise of American civil servants in the 1960s. Standy probably had a wife and kids in Scarborough. He looked like he should be playing football or serving in the Marines. He struck Cerise as the type of man who kidded himself about who he really was. All the park stuff, the sly secluded cock-suckings, this was all on the down-low. He didn't tell anybody about it, not even his closest friend, whom he was probably wretchedly in love with.

OK, so Cerise liked to make up stories about people. She might be totally wrong about these guys, but if she'd learned one thing while researching the 'cruising' scene, it was that nobody asked questions. When one guy met another in the park, he didn't say, 'Hey, let me buy you a drink.' They didn't chat, didn't ask names or relationship statuses. Cruising was all about sex.

And Cerise wanted in on it.

Her backpack weighed her down, keeping her from flipping over. She felt like a turtle that couldn't regain its footing, but she didn't need to be on her feet right now. All she wanted was Crouchy's cock between her lips.

'What are you doing?' Crouchy gasped as Cerise traced her hand up his lean thigh. 'Who the hell are you?'

'Don't ask,' she said, finding his fat cock underneath his skinny jeans. 'Just let me. Please? Let me suck it.'

Crouchy looked up at Standy with severe apprehension marking his brow. She could see them both fairly well now, but Standy was critically hard to read. Did he want to fuck her or punch her? Or did he just want her to go the hell away so he could bring his dick out of hiding? The mystery made her heart drop into her lungs.

'Is this some kind ohe some kf a trick?' Standy asked, and Cerise nearly jumped because his voice surprised her so. It wasn't rough and gruff like she'd anticipated, based solely on his jaw and haircut and Toronto Maple Leafs jacket. No, this big strong man spoke with a definite gay guy lisp, and it pleased her to no end. Maybe there was no wife in the suburbs for Standy. Maybe he was every bit as out and loud and proud as she thought Crouchy must be. Maybe Cerise shouldn't judge a book by his square jaw.

'No tricks,' Cerise said, first looking Standy in the eye and then shifting her attention to Crouchy. Oh, his pale skin and raven hair made her tremble. There was something about this guy that reminded her of Professor MacLaren, even though they looked nothing alike. He hadn't moved her hand away from his hard cock, and she *rubbed it gently through his jeans. 'Look, I'll be honest: I'm researching a book.'*

'A book?' Standy asked. 'What the hell kind of book?'

Cerise took a deep breath. 'Sorry, that's a stupid excuse. The truth is that I'm cruising, just like you.'

Crouchy and Standy exchanged looks, and Cerise wondered if they believed her.

'I'm crazy,' she told them. Tears filled her eyes, though she had no idea where they'd come from. 'I'm only attracted to men who like men. It's totally insane, being me. It's so frustrating. You have no idea.'

'Awww,' the lean, pale guy sighed. 'Poor baby.'

'Poor sweet baby,' the tall guy joined in. After a moment, he unzipped his fly and pulled out his immense erection. To Crouchy, he said, 'Let the girl suck your cock while you work on mine.'

Cerise couldn't help staring. It had been a very long time since she'd seen a dick in the flesh. On her computer screen? Streaming gay porn? Sure, all the time. If her cramped little office's walls could talk, they'd stammer, 'Gay sex ... so much gay sex!' But a fat, erect cock in real life? It had been years since she'd taken one in her mouth. Not that she had trepidations. Giving head was like riding a bike.

Crouchy's face looked ghostly as he unzipped his jeans. They were so tight he had to wriggle his hips as he pushed them down his thighs. No underwear. Cerise could have fainted at the sight of his alabaster dick straining from a bed of dark pubic hair. His balls were nearly bare, and they hung heavy beneath his beautiful cock.

It could have been a statue, museum quality. Crouchy's erection was beyond beautiful. Cerise couldn't get over how straight it was, big and bold and arrow-straight. No bulging veins, at least not that she could see. The tip was wonderfully smooth and glistening with pre-cum – that, she could see very well.

'It's all yours,' Crouchy said, holding his dick by the base. 'I thought you wanted to suck it.'

'I do,' Cerise whispered. 'Yes.'

Her throat ran dry, and she tried to swallow but there was nothing.

'I thought you wanted to suck this,' Standy said to Crouchy, then smacked the guy's gaunt cheek with his thick, hard cock. The wet slapping brought a pulse between Cerise's legs. 'Go on. Suck it.'

Cerise and her boy-crush obeyed in unison, both launching themselves at the cocks in front of them. When Cerise wrapped her lips around Crouchy's dick he moaned around Standy's. At the top of their little pyramid of cocksucking, Standy grunted and jerked. He sent two big hands through Crouchy's dark hair and fucked that gaunt face slowly. Cerise had the best seat in the house, with a bottom-up ns.a bottoview of the big guy's cock pumping like a piston in and out of the smaller guy's mouth. God, those lips looked so pink against his white skin, like they'd been painted on.

Cerise wondered if she looked half as sexy sucking Crouchy's dick, though, she had to admit, she was distracted by the sight of cocksucking above her. Redoubling her efforts, she turned her face to Crouchy's crotch and sucked his dick slow and steady. That was her method of choice. Sure it might look impressive if she deepthroated him the way he was deepthroating Standy, but she remembered the gagging pang of taking a cock that far in. She'd gag and sputter and pull away with bleary eyes and mucous saturating her nostrils and her throat. How unsexy was that?

Lying on her back, propped up by the books and papers and laptop in her pack, Cerise wrapped her fist around Crouchy's fine marble cock and sucked the tip while she pumped the shaft. By the focused look on his face, she wouldn't have known he was getting any pleasure from her actions at all. His belly told the whole story, though. Just above the dark line of his pubic hair, his pelvis jumped and twinged as she sucked him off.

The thing that most intrigued Cerise about cruising, whether it was present-day or back in the 1920s, was that it was truly about scratching an itch. Cruising was different than one-night stands, where a guy picked up another guy in a bar. In that situation, a person would look around until they spotted someone they were at least moderately attracted to, depending on their level of drunkenness.

In the park, you couldn't be so picky. If you're a toppy sort of guy and you stumble across a bottom, you feed him your cock. If you're looking to open your mouth to some random guy, anyone will do. It had almost nothing to do with attraction. Cerise didn't harbour any misguided beliefs that these men were attracted to her. They'd put up a bit of a fight because she wasn't a guy, but at the end of the day she was just another willing mouth. They didn't have to be attracted to her. That part didn't matter.

One hundred years ago, the park was a destination for men who had sex with men because there were significantly fewer places for them to get off together. Now, gay men had legal rights, marriage rights, housing rights, and on and on. The park was still about getting off, but more about the novelty of doing it in a public space, the danger of getting caught, and following in the footsteps of gay men throughout the ages.

Ultimately, beyond all academics, sucking and fucking in the park had one main goal: orgasm. Cerise was ridiculously, school-girlishly drawn to the pale vampire whose cock pulsed against her tongue, but she knew that, realistically, he probably wasn't attracted to her. She probably meant nothing to him. But so what? The park was all about meet-ups in the dark, surrendering and succumbing without ever getting a clear look at the guy whose cock was throbbing in your mouth. After all, you didn't want to recognise him tomorrow morning when you walked by each other on the subway platform.

In the park, everything was anonymous. No faces, no names.

Cerise tightened her fist around Crouchy's delicious dick. She sucked it hard enough to get him moaning. As she bobbed against his crotch, his cock spilled massive pools of pre-cum against her tongue. It wouldn't be long before he opened the floodgates and released torrents of cum down her throat. His dick tasted like sweat and denim. What would his cream taste like?

She sucked hard, devoting every bit of strength to bringing this beautiful gay guy to orgasm. Maybe he'd only come to the park to get someone else off, but Crouchy was in for a treat tonight. Cerise stroked him off whilen him off she worked him with her mouth, so that her fist met her lips with every go. She could feel the pressure build, the suction intensify. Judging by the strain in his bony jaw, he was close.

With her free hand, Cerise brushed her fingers across Crouchy's tightened balls, and that little change in sensation did the trick. Flicking his hair and leaning back, he bucked into Cerise's mouth so deep she nearly choked.

His cream met her tongue in constant floods of dense, musky heat. She swallowed because she didn't want to be rude, and the aftertaste was pleasantly sweet. More came, more cum, and she sucked that down, too. The texture was lovely, like rich, smooth pudding. It kept coming, and she kept swallowing, burst after burst. She didn't want to think about this encounter ending, because the concept made her listless and sad.

When Crouchy stole his spent cock from between her lips, she immediately missed his girth between her tongue and the roof of her mouth. Nothing to do now but lie back and stare at the rabid cocksucking overhead. Her new crush devoured the big guy's dick, getting her face wet and messy with droplets of pre-cum and saliva. Standy had the base of his erection in hand, and rubbed it with the pad of his thumb while Crouchy ate the tip and most of that fat shaft.

When Standy cradled his big balls in a hammock of fingers, Cerise knew he was ready to come. He jostled his nuts, and that got him panting. Crouchy's lips curled into a neat smile as the big guy fucked his face. They both growled, and the force of that sound echoed through Cerise's groin. She was so close that all it would take was a tap at her clit. Could she let herself come in front of strangers? In a park after dark? Fooling around on the ground?

Standy took a step back just as Cerise sucked in her belly and snuck her fingers under the waist of her jeans. The man on top fucked his fist so fast his hand was just a blur. Her lovely boy responded by sticking out his tongue, creating a target for top.

Cerise squirmed on the ground, forcing her fingers past her pubic hair until finally, finally she found her clit. She pressed down hard on her sweet, sensitive bud, urging it in tight circles beneath the closed fly of her jeans. 'Yes,' she whispered, staring up at that fat cock in a fierce fist. 'Yes, come!'

Her body obeyed, and so did Standy's. They came at once, she on the ground, he in the air. His cream shot over her in thick ropes. The first few spurts landed on Crouchy's big pink tongue, and the next few fell short, spreading hot across her chin and neck.

The pleasure of being hit with a gay man's cum brought Cerise to a higher level of orgasm. She scoured her clit, up and down now, until her climax peaked again. The men were both looking at her now, and she wanted to smile, but she had to clench her teeth to keep from crying out. Maybe she'd read too many court reports, but she didn't want to get caught in such a compromising position.

Quiet, quiet! Don't cry out! Bury that scream!

Cerise bit her lip and breathed through her nose until she could speak without gasping. The men had already packed up their cocks. They seemed ready to go, and all she could think to say was, 'Thank you.'

The men looked at each other and nodded. 'You too,' they both said.

'Well, see you around,' the big guy said before shuffling up the incline and onto the lit path.

Just like that, he was gone.

The other guy didn't seem so eager to flee the scene, and that warmed Cerise's heart. As she pulled her hand from her pants, he said, 'I'm goinherI'mg to the subway. You heading that way?'

Cerise nodded, feeling suddenly bashful. Cruising etiquette said they should each go their separate ways, but she felt so attached to this guy. She'd just sucked his dick after all. 'Subway? Yeah.'

Pulling a tissue from his pocket, Crouchy mopped up the warm cum from her face and neck. They both laughed nervously as he helped her to her feet. It was dangerous, walking through the park with a guy she didn't know. He could be anyone. All she knew about him was that he sucked dick and he was breathtakingly cute.

But Cerise had a good feeling about this boy. This could be the start of a beautiful friendship … with benefits?

Pulparazzi
Heather Towne

'I was yours when our eyes met,' Katalina san Crescenda breathed, brushing a copper tendril of hair away from Reg 'Prof' Wildman's high, bronzed forehead.

He grunted, flake-gold eyes hard and knowing, full, cynical lips parting in a grim smile. He reached out and grasped Katalina's trembling shoulders in his huge, able hands, and she thrilled with the kiln-heat of his bold passion – her passion.

Her amber eyes glowed like Nubian gems from beneath her hooded eyelids, as the big man moved his stone-cut head inexorably forward, moist, rugged lips meeting, then pressing into Katalina's petalled lips. She threw her arms around him, willingly, gladly offering up everything she had to offer to the globetrotting scientist and adventurer, sworn enemy of evil.

Reg 'Prof' Wildman devoured the enraptured woman's

sensuous mouth, spanning, industrious hands sliding down her rounded shoulders and around her curved back. Setting the raven-haired contessa's senses to singing the praises of the burnished, brainy man of a thousand gizmos and gadgets like never before. He fingered Katalina's bra strap with his blunt, nimble digits, finding the clasp that unlocked the twin treasures of her heaving chest and ...

Fumbling, pinching my skin, scratching my back. 'Oh, for goodness sakes, let me, Milton!' I finally exhaled, snapping my eyes open and shattering my dream-date.

'Uh, yeah, OK, Katie,' Milton gulped in relief. He pulled his sweaty, freckled hands away, his bony face red as his hair.

I reached back and easily unfastened my bra like the Chinese puzzle it wasn't. Milton's a nice guy, not too bad-looking if you ignore the overbite, but it seemed like no amount of fevered imagining on my part was going to turn the gangly geek into he-man actioner Reg 'Prof' Wildman, pulp-style hero of the Rough Paper Renegade series of books, authored by Dan D. Cannon.

But a girl could still fantasise ...

'Tear my clothes off, you brute! Ravage me as you will!' I wailed, as Cassandra von Hellemonton had wailed in *Black Cloud of Bengali Terror*.

Milton just stared at me, bulging Adam's apple running up and down his scrawny neck, thin lips mouthing, 'Whaaat?'

So I pulled my sweater up over my head, threw my bra away, strew the useless garments about. Baring my pale, quivering, pink-tipped breasts to the stricken man. I flung my dark-framed glasses aside and shook out my night-shaded tresses, Milton's jaw-dropped face blurring the way I like it. I thrust out my handful heapings of woman-flesh, nipples pointing flinty as the arrowheads in *Thundering Plains of Purple Pestilence*. Ththeen I held my breath, waiting, yearning ... waiting.

I grabbed Milton's hands and planted them on my boobs. 'Yeeess!' I moaned, squeezing the clammy hands so that they squeezed my brimming boobs. 'Suck on my bosoms as you sucked poison out of the neck of Rachel El Antaari in *Yellow Desert of Devastation*!'

I grabbed Milton's knobby shoulders and jerked him forward, plastering his fiery face against my throbbing chest. And when he did nothing – again – I plugged a buzzing nipple into his open mouth and begged him to suck.

He choked, coughed, kind of sucked, staring up at me with his cow eyes. I gripped his jutting ears and roughly guided his head over to my other needful nipple. And he tentatively mouthed that, as well. His arms and hands now dangling at his sides limp as the slain court jester in *White Atomic War over Antarctica*.

I sighed and shoved the guy back. Then stood up and stripped off my jeans and panties, still entertaining some faint hope of some small measure of satisfaction.

I stood over the supine software sales associate on the couch, my nude, lewd, creamy-white body gleaming in the flickering light of the Transformers movie playing on the television like the ornate, obscenely carved ivory pillars of the heathen temple gleamed in *Scarlet Sacrifice to the Space Gods*. My glistening breasts rose and fell like the storm-swollen seas in *Green Galleons of Sargasso Slaughter*, furred pussy dark and moist and dense as the steaming jungles in *Abattoir for the Ebony Amazonians*.

But Milton just gazed up at me, dazed and confused. I groaned and dropped to my knees in the shag, deftly unbelted and unzipped the awestruck man-child, his holstered iPhone catching on the couch cushions as I yanked his corduroy Dockers down.

His prick was soft with shock, resting shrivelled in a nest of ginger pubes. I brazenly grabbed onto it and pulled on it. And it rose up in my warm, insistent hand, like the deadly king cobra emerging from its wicker basket lair in Prince Zazeem's palace in *Armageddon of the Violet Twilight*. Milton managed to prop himself up on shaking elbows and watch me stroke his cock to its full height and width and glory.

'K-Katie!' he gasped, his entire stick-figure shaking now.

But I wasn't Katie. Not the shy, sincere stock girl from the Cover's big box bookstore. I was Helena de Carillon-Velarez, warrior noble lady who held Reg 'Prof'

Wildman's vibrating broadsword in her mailed fist and defied the chiselled giant to wrest it free in the time-travel medieval epic *Lavender Legions of Hell and Gone*.

I swirled my hand up and down Milton's straining, purple-capped pole, feeling the raw power of his pulsating need all through me, my pussy dripping elation into the shag. Then I looked the squirming guy square in the boggled eyes and parted my crimson lips and bent my silky neck and took his mushroomed hood, his boiling shaft, into my warm, wet, wicked mouth. Drinking of the man as the golden fawn drank of the mirror-like mountain waters in *Burnt-Orange Forest War Forever*.

Milton yelped. Jerked. Blew hot semen against the roof of my mouth and down my throat – without warning.

I yanked his spurting prick out of my mouth before I drowned. And caught cum in the eye, up my nose. Abandoning all hope of Milton Werton ever possessing the strength, stamina, and savage sexual prowess of one Reg 'Prof' Wildman.

* * *

The author of the Rough Paper Renegade chronicles, Dan D. Cannon, was just as mysterin mt as myous a figure as pulp hero Reg 'Prof' Wildman himself. Pictured on the backs of the books only in shadowy silhouette, a glowing cigarette tip within the darkened outline shedding no light on the subject whatsoever; the biographical blurb stating only that Dan was a pulpwood magazine and pulp hero enthusiast – like myself – possessing a vast collection of the rough-edged, high-acid paper magazines from the 20s, 30s, and 40s at some secret location.

I'd gotten hooked on the pulps in my teens, when I'd been willed my grandfather's three-hundred-strong collection. Cracking open the glossy, blazingly lurid, four-colour covers and reading the rollicking prose bursting with red-hot action and snap-crackling dialogue had thrilled me then – and now.

I'd devoured all the genres – from Adventure to Zeppelin – in great, pulpy chunks. But my favourites were the 'hero pulps': Doc Savage, The Shadow, The Spider, Operator No. 5; with their tough, witty, handsome – male and female – characters, outlandish plots, exotic locales, and kazillion gadgets. Earth-shakers and heartbreakers who used their muscle, guile, and scientific know-how to rescue the world from the evil clutches of all manner of diabolical madmen, weekly, monthly, and quarterly.

And when Dan D. Cannon came along, blazing a new trail through the old pulp jungle with Reg 'Prof' Wildman, I lapped it up like the American Grub Street presses used to lap up hardwood.

So, after cleaning Milton and myself off – the couch, carpet, and ceiling – I told the spent, quick-trigger nerd that our trip to the Microsoft TechEd Convention was a

no-go. I was embarking on a heroic quest of my own –
to locate the like-minded spirit who I was certain could
fully satisfy me and my pulp fiction, and friction, crav-
ings: Dan D. Cannon.

* * *

I phoned the publisher of the Rough Paper Renegade
books, Purple Prose Publications. They were no help,
citing a 'confidentiality agreement'. I trolled the Web for
articles, interviews, book signings, sightings … anything
about the elusive Dan D. Cannon. And got nothing. I
peppered the online pulp magazine discussion groups
with pleas for help. To no avail.

Forcing me to leave my sleepy Southwestern town and
journey by bus to the ink-stained centre of publishing, the
beating heart of the modern-day pulp rebirth, hallowed
home of Purple Prose Publications: New York City!

The receptionist at triple-P's 42nd Street office was
uncooperative. Downright rude, when she caught me
leafing through the morning mail on her desk after she'd
gone to the washroom. Ditto the editors I accosted.

But I was not to be stopped. Just as Reg 'Prof' Wildman
was never stopped in his two-fisted crusades for justice,
or vengeance, or a missing damsel or diamond. I simply
held my nose and dove into the dumpster in back of the
building; started sifting through sacks of trash.

Until, at last, I found a clue to the identity of my favourite pulp fiction writer in the whole wide world: a voided cheque listing Dan D. Cannon as Payee, an address in Brooklyn printed just below!

It was a used bookstore, 'Paperbackers', located in a two-storey building built at the turn of the last century. And as I pushed through the glass-panelled front door, my nose and senses were assailed by that yellowed paper smell that always sets my spine to tingling. 'Got any pulps?' I asked the woman behind the polished oak counter, playing it cagey, casing the joint.

Until I spotted the humungous section of Rough Paper Renegade books. And went slightly ga-ga.

All sixteen stories in the series were there, first edition hardcovers and softcovers, foreign editions, omnibus editions thick as New York phone books, juicy as New York steaks. My starry eyes and twitching fingers danced all over the glossy, garish spines and covers that only hinted at the excitement inside.

'Fan of Dan D. Cannon?' the woman asked rhetorically, suddenly right behind me.

'Huge fan!' I gushed, marvelling at a mapback edition of *Death Rays from the Ultraviolet Underworld*.

She lightly touched my shoulder. 'Perhaps you'd like to explore the inspiration for all those books – in the pulp vault?'

The very words took my breath away.

She guided me through book-lined aisles to the rear of the store, along a dimly lit hallway, down a rickety flight of stairs that led to a subterranean basement. There she grated back the foot-thick door of an ancient bank vault and ushered me inside.

I stood in the eerie darkness, trembling. Until the woman brushed by and pulled on a chain, casting light on the contents of that massive, underground ossuary. And what content!

The shelves of the vault were stacked with row after row of pulp magazines in protective polyurethane jacket slips, the spines screaming out: Doc Savage, The Phantom Detective, Secret Agent X, and every other genre from Air Action to Zippy Stories. I stared, wide-eyed, at the wondrous collection, face flushing and glasses fogging.

The woman pulled down a selection of Fine and Very Good + pulps and laid them out on the wooden table in the middle of the vault. 'Let me take your coat,' she said. 'You look hot.'

She slid my coat off my shoulders and draped it over a chair. Then gripped my bare arms and vainly tried to rub out the goose bumps with her warm, caressing hands. 'Would you like to ... meet Dan D. Cannon?' she breathed into my burning bright ear.

I spun around in her arms, desperately searching her flake-gold eyes. 'Yes! Oh, yes! That's what I've come to New York for!'

'Well, mission accomplished.' She smiled. 'I'm Danielle "Dan" D. Cannon, author of the Rough Paper Renegade books.'

I gasped, gaped, my composure as tattered as a 'reading copy' pulp. She was maybe forty years of age, with short, copper-coloured hair and a strong, handsome, tanned face. She was wearing a sleeveless blue blouse that showed off her lean, muscled arms and high, full breasts, a pair of black pants that fit snug to her slender legs and trim waist. She could've been Reg 'Prof' Wildman's sister!

'And now that you know,' she murmured, 'I'll have to seal your lips to secrecy.'

And she kissed me – on the lips!

I went all warm and woozy, my skinny legs quivering in my skinny jeans, my nipples springing out and almost parting the stitching of my short-sleeved sweater. She was Dan D. Cannon! I was surrounded by pulp! And … she'd just kissed me!

Kissed me again. Harder this time, smack on my dangling lips. Like Reg 'Prof' Wildman had kissed Mayabelle Mumphries on board his yacht, the *Scallywag*, in *Destruction Rises Blue from the Deeps*.

Her tongue slid into my mouth, touched and tangled with my tongue. And I grabbed back at her, the two of us fitting together hot and tight and perfectly, like a Wildman action plan. The muscles on her back writhed like serpents under my grasping hands, as she clutched at my dark tresses. As we anxiously fed on each other's mouths, tongues flashiy bngues fng together.

The temperature in the vault soared along with my body temp, my glasses steaming up again in the erotic embrace. Danielle tried to take them off, but I shook my head 'no'. I wanted to see everything that went on, all those glorious pulps. She caught my tongue between her strong, white teeth as I tried to explain, sucked on the slippery pink appendage, her nimble fingers combing through my hair.

She tore my sweater out of my jeans and up over my head, casting the garment aside. Then she kissed me again, Frenched me again, reaching behind my back and easily unfastening my bra, dragging it away. She knew her way around such gadgets, all right.

I shuddered with sheer delight as Danielle caught my bare breasts in her able hands and cupped and squeezed them. Dropped her head down and swirled her knowing tongue all around first one rigid, reaching nipple, and then the other. Until the pink buds stuck out shiny and painfully erect in the light – like me.

She captured one of the engorged tips in her mouth and sucked on it. I yelped, 'Sweet gadzooks!' Quoting Reg 'Prof' Wildman's spunky sidekick and sometime love interest, Sara-Beth Cummins, when faced with amazement.

Danielle sucked and sucked on my buzzing nipples,

bringing me to my toes, my body vibrating with wicked pleasure. She pushed my boobs together and slashed her wet tongue across both nipples at once. Then bit into the straining pointers with her sharp teeth, almost shooting me through the metal ceiling on the bolt of electricity that arced all through my body.

My pussy was a molten pool in my jeans. Which Danielle sensed with a woman's intuition, reaching down and rubbing my jeaned crotch. Causing me to cry out as the disbelieving tribespeople cried out at the living incarnations of the gods they prayed to in *Crimson Spirits of the Bloody Blade*.

I staggered back against the table, Danielle clutching, swallowing up and sucking my breasts, rubbing my pussy, taking no prisoners in her stunning sexual onslaught. She unhanded me only long enough to strip away her top and bottom, her sculpted body spilling out burnished bronze, golden mounds topped by tan, taut nipples, pussy shaved bare, folds glistening ripe and juicy.

I touched her breasts, traced the silken skin with shaking fingers. Then grasped and squeezed her heated jugs of plenty. She tilted her head back and moaned, as I latched onto her rubbery nipples and rolled.

I grew suddenly and stunningly bolder, brazen, gripping her more than handful breasts and kneading them, working them with my hot little hands. Then I bent my head down and pushed her breasts up, tickled an engorged nipple with the tip of my outstretched tongue. And she shuddered, her boobs jumping in my clutching hands.

I tongued her other nipple, teasing it even higher and harder. I swirled my tongue all around and over the blossomed buds, tasting the pebbly width of her areolae, the rubbery texture of her nipples. Eagerly, anxiously bobbing my head back and forth between her breasts, I spun my tongue all around her nipples, bathing them in my saliva; making her shiver with delight and me surge with confidence, making them shine.

She moaned when I flogged her nipples with my tongue, gasped when I sunk my teeth into the delicious protuberances. I bit into one, the other one, pulling on them, stretching them out between my teeth. Before sealing my lips around, and sucking. I was reckless, ravenous.

Danielle grabbed onto my head and clutched me close to her heaving chest, as I sucked hard and tight on one nipple, then the other. They filled my mouth, engorged and throbbing. I tugged on them, my cheeks bing my cheillowing, nursing on the woman's beautiful boobs, ablaze with flaming pulpmistress passion.

I inhaled as much of her one tit as I could and pulled on the succulent mass. Then I disgorged that tit, shining and dripping, swallowed half of her other breast, vacuuming the ripe flesh, tweaking her nipple with my tongue.

Before pushing both of her mounds together and slashing my tongue across both of her nipples at once. She'd taught me well, already, because she moaned, her tits and body trembling in my hands. I crammed her nipples into my mouth and sucked on them together.

Finally, after getting almost my fill of her boobs and nipples, I let go of them. I stared at the mauled masses, their glistening tips, my own breasts bobbing up and down as excitedly as hers.

I dropped down to my knees, in-between her strong legs. I was at the temple of the High Priestess of Pulp. I *had* to worship.

Her pussy was sodden, dripping with moisture, lips swollen. I stuck out my tongue and touched her flaps with the tip.

'Oh!' she gasped, jerking.

I gloried in her response, grew ever bolder, sliding my hands around her thighs and onto the taut, twin mounds of her butt cheeks, digging my fingernails into the smooth, stretched skin. Then I gulped air and courage and thrust my tongue out and licked up her pussy from deep in-between her legs to the top of her slit, dragging her sex in one long, hard, wet stroke.

She spasmed, her bum and body jumping in my sweaty, clinging hands.

Danielle grabbed up her shivering breasts and squeezed them, staring down at me, quivering. I looked up at her and quavered a grin, my lips slick with her juices. Then I licked her again, and again. I lapped her pussy, stroking her flaps with my tongue, scooping up her tangy essence and swallowing it down.

She slid her hands forward on her breasts and captured her jutting nipples between her fingers, rolled them, pulled them. As I tongued her repeatedly.

Until I jerked my head back and smacked my lips. Then I spread her pussy lips wide with my fingers, exposing her shining pink, swollen clit. I blew on her clit, making her shudder. I fashioned my tongue into a pink blade and speared it inside of her. 'God!' she cried, jolted by the impact of my tongue in her pussy.

I was on fire, blazing with lust like the red-hot magma blazed molten in *Ochre Ogres of the Underworld*. I pistoned my head back and forth, pumping Danielle, flat-out fucking her with my stuck-out tongue. Before burying it inside of her and squirming it around, digging deep into her steaming treasure box. She bent over almost in two, overcome with emotion.

I reeled my tongue out of her tunnel and licked her flaps again. Then I kissed her clit, then engulfed it with my lips and sucked on the swollen button. She bucked, her buttocks rippling under my grasping hands. I vacuum-sealed her clit, my cheeks billowing. She pulsed in my mouth, shaking with a passion almost as powerful as mine.

'Enough foreplay!' she suddenly snarled, jerking me up and shoving me backwards onto the table.

I landed with a splat on the pulps. Followed by my panties landing with a splat somewhere far off, after Danielle peeled away my jeans and underwear. She slid me further up the table. Then mounted the table and me, our naked bodies melding together with the heat of a thousand suns.

She smothered me with her mouth, her heavy breasts pressing into my breasts, our pussies kissing together in-between my spread legs, hot and wet and delicious. She started moving hnd ted mover hips, pumping her pussy into my pussy. Making reckless, passionate love to me like Reg 'Prof' Wildman had made reckless, passionate love to Scarlett Mulvavery on the loamy banks of the River Avonmore in *The Emerald Invasion*.

Danielle pushed one of my legs up for better positioning, then met my pussy with her pussy in a heated, squishy, more-direct embrace, pumping her powerful hips again. I dug my fingernails into the flesh of her flexing butt cheeks and urged her on, the grinding of gashes flooding me with liquid fire.

The table groaned and screeched like the pair of us, the pulps in their plastic casings squeaking back and forth under our surging bodies, the spicy smell of incendiary sex suffusing the sweating vault. I stuck out my tongue and licked at a flying nipple, Danielle's hanging breasts swaying in rhythm to her frantic pussy-rubbing. She pumped me even harder, faster, spurred on by my claws in her clenching cheeks, my teeth locking onto a stiffened jutter.

The wet-hot friction became unbearable. My clit and body swelled to the bursting point. 'Ohmigod, I'm coming!' I screamed. Imitating no one but myself in my most intimate moments.

Danielle gritted her teeth and savagely ground our smouldering pussies into flames.

A shockwave of pure, white-hot joy slammed through my jumping body. As Danielle's red velvet mouth broke open in a silent scream, her sweat-sheened body spasming. We clutched each other, rocking with orgasmic ecstasy, over and over and over.

A thrilling, truly X-rated pulpy conclusion to my heroic quest for the talented Dan D. Cannon.

* * *

I work at Paperbackers now, live in New York City. Danielle's teaching me the tricks of the pulp writing trade, the formulas and gimmicks she uses to plot, people, and produce a rip-roaring Reg 'Prof' Wildman adventure yarn. Someday I hope to ghostwrite one. If I can ever tear myself away from that pulp vault.

The Portcullis
Rose de Fer

Morlech Castle is ominous and beautiful in the moonlight. The bluish glow casts strange, distorted shadows against the weathered stone walls of the ruined portions and glints like cold fire in the leaded windows of the intact keep. All around us the trees whisper with sinister promise in the faint breeze. Otherwise the night is silent, filled with ancient secrets.

Suddenly a loud *POP!* breaks the stillness. I give a startled little cry and then clap my hands over my mouth to stifle the near-hysterical fit of giggles that follows.

'Nervous?' Charles asks with a knowing smile.

He holds the bottle out to me and I take it, slurping at the ice-cold bubbles that stream down the neck and over my hand.

'Very,' I confess.

I drink some more champagne and sigh with pleasure at

the taste. It is our little tradition. Champagne at midnight in the grounds of the castle where we met. That was six years ago. At the time we'd both been alone. Very bored, very lonely and very horny.

* * *

After roaming aimlessly through the cold empty rooms of the castle for an hour or so, I'd suddenly got the feeling that I was being watched. I felt followed all along the crumbling curtain walls, as though some predator were pacing along behind me. Footsteps echoed behind me in theple narrow spiral stairwell as I climbed up to the ramparts. I caught a whiff of cologne as I made my way along the walkway, trying to focus on the spectacular view spread out below me.

When I finally turned to confront my stalker, any sense of outrage vanished immediately. He was gorgeous. Older than me by ten years or so, with chiselled aristocratic features and eyes so deep and dark they were almost black. There was something otherworldly about him, something that promised excitement and even danger. My bold confrontation died on my lips as he smiled disarmingly and asked if I'd like to join him for lunch. It was all I could do to stammer out a meek 'yes'. In fact, it was probably 'Oh, yes'.

Lunch was a decadent feast in a nearby Italian

restaurant. The afternoon of food, wine and chocolate led to an evening of steamy sex in Charles's hotel room. I called in sick to work the next morning so we could spend the day together. And that night we waited until midnight and sneaked back into the grounds with a bottle of champagne. The cork exploded from the bottle like a gunshot fired at the moon, but no one heard and no one came. We stretched out under the stars and talked long into the night, drunk on the bubbly and each other.

I had never had sex outside before. The night was crisp and cold and I shivered in Charles's arms as he pushed me down on the grass and fucked me. With long slow strokes he slid in and out of me, fitting perfectly one moment and then leaving me bereft the next. I soon lost my inhibitions, wrapping my legs tightly around him, digging my heels into his arse as I urged him deeper, harder, faster. I sent a wild cry up into the night sky as he wrenched the first of several powerful climaxes from me. Neither of us could pinpoint the moment when lust became love but we were left wondering if the ancient site retained some residual magic.

* * *

'What is it you're afraid of, Amy?' Charles asks, bringing me back to the present.

He reaches for the bottle, I pass it back to him and he

swigs heartily from it. I smile as I watch him. We'd done the same thing at our wedding, swept up in the joy and madness of the whole extravagant event. We'd sneaked away from the party for a stolen quickie up against a tree in the churchyard, leaving the guests hungry and impatient and wondering where we could have gone.

'We've never been caught,' he reminds me.

'I know, but ...'

His eyes shine with wicked intent. 'But what?'

I blush and kick at the grass, feeling silly, childish, overwhelmed, out of my depth. 'What if someone sees?'

'Then they see.'

He's determined not to give me any shred of comfort. Since the day we met he's delighted in wrong-footing me, in pushing me to the edge and then just beyond.

Instead of Niagara Falls or Hawaii or any of the other traditional romantic hotspots, he'd taken me to Transylvania for our honeymoon. We went climbing in the Carpathian Mountains and stayed in a castle rumoured to have been Dracula's. For our first anniversary we went skydiving over the Sonoran desert. For our second, snowboarding in the Alps. So I was no stranger to adventure. My life until meeting Charles had been bland and safe, with little to make my heart pound. Afterwards, I felt alive. Truly alive.

But the adventures weren't all about flirtations with danger. Sometimes they were as simple as testing my limits. The first time he tied me up I was terrified. I liked his dominance but the thought of being so completely helpless was almost more than I co Coreked awauld take. It was hard to submit, to allow myself to be bound hand and foot to the lavish four-poster bed in the honeymoon suite. I trusted him, of course, and once I was naked and splayed out before him like that, I found the loss of control exhilarating.

He teased me, caressing every inch of my exposed flesh, cruelly avoiding the places that wanted his attention most of all. He raised goose bumps as he trailed his fingers along my thighs and up my sides, circling my breasts. I writhed in my bonds, aching for him as he kissed a line down my body, at last flicking his tongue over my sensitive nipples. Blood roared in my ears and my sex throbbed so hard it was almost painful. When he finally entered me, thrusting himself up to the hilt, it took only seconds before I was racked with the spasms of a shattering orgasm.

My sex life was never the same after that.

One afternoon he surprised me with a pair of handcuffs. He ambushed me in the bedroom, threw me onto the bed and cuffed my wrists behind my back. He yanked my skirt up, tore my knickers off and stuffed them in my mouth. Then he fisted a hand in my hair roughly and growled in my ear that I was not to resist, that any disobedience would be severely punished.

I had never been so wet in my life. My face burned with shame and excitement as he bent me over the bed and fucked me hard and fast. I screamed into my gag, relishing the freedom of knowing that no one could hear me. I struggled a little and he slapped my arse sharply. The pain only intensified my arousal and I begged him for more by pretending to resist. He smacked me again, each stinging slap making me want more. When my arse was warm and tingling he filled me with his cock, again and again. I clenched myself tightly around it, delighting in his own little noises of pleasure. I came as soon as he wedged his hands underneath me to pinch my clit.

That night he took me out to dinner and I wore a short-sleeved dress to display the vivid red marks left by the handcuffs. The waiter looked startled for a moment before regaining his composure and my smile must have reassured him that I wasn't a victim. A co-worker asked me about the marks the next day and it was clear she didn't believe my silly lie. It was also clear she felt she was missing out on something.

Over the years that followed I cherished every bruise and welt Charles left on my body. I watched them fade a little each day until they were gone and he could leave me with new ones. But I never lost my fear. It was the drug that kept me coming back for more. I needed the terror, the sense of losing control.

'Are you afraid of the pain?' Charles asks.

I take another gulp of champagne and nod meekly. I had never known pain could be erotic, had never suspected that I had such a submissive and masochistic nature. Charles had awakened me to so many unfamiliar sensual delights. But his plan for tonight has me terrified. It's not just about pain and submission; tonight he has promised to push me further.

'You'll be a good girl, though,' he says coolly, opening the leather holdall he brought with him. 'You'll make me proud.'

I close my eyes, knowing what's inside it but still afraid to look. I hear the heavy clink of metal and I press my thighs together. Already my knickers are soaked. I'm dizzy with the rush of conflicting emotions. How is it possible to be so frightened and yet so aroused at the same time? How is it possible to want what you absolutely don't want? And then to love it and want it all over again?

None of the questions matter, though. All that matters is the moment, the heady thrill of relinquishing control to someone you trust wholly and absolutely.

'It's time, Amy.'

I hesitate for only a moment. Then, trembling, I sink to my knees on the ground and lower my head. There is the rustle of his footsteps in the grass as he approaches, then the jingle of chains. I lift my hair out of the way and wince at the chill of steel against my neck. He locks my heavy collar into place. Its weight is both intimidating and comforting. It makes me feel utterly powerless. While I wear it, I am truly a slave.

'Raise your arms,' he says.

I obey, keeping my eyes closed. He gently slips my dress off over my head and unhooks my bra. My nipples stiffen at their exposure to the night air and I feel my sense of submission deepen. My body can't hide its arousal, a fact that makes me feel even more at Charles's mercy.

He strokes my head and I nuzzle his leg like a puppy, pleading silently for him to spare me. I know he won't. I also know I don't really want him to. But it's all part of the dance. A dance usually done in private, behind closed doors. But not this time. Not tonight.

'Give me your wrists.'

Opening my eyes at last, I hold out my trembling hands and try to stay still as he fastens the cold metal shackles around my slender wrists. I might be a prisoner of the Inquisition or a captured princess sold into slavery in the Ottoman Empire. But no fantasy will save me from the reality of what's about to happen.

Charles takes pity on me and kisses me, stroking my bare back and telling me what a good girl I am. The words always make me melt. They're like a magic charm that gives me the courage not to beg my way out of it. Because, secretly, I want it as much as he does. My total surrender is the key to bliss – for both of us.

He crouches beside me and takes my knickers down.

I obediently lift one leg at a time so he can slip them off and he tucks them into his pocket with a smile. Then he locks another pair of shackles around my ankles. A short chain connects them so I can open my legs wide enough to walk but not run. Not that I would ever run.

I'm too frightened to feel the exhilaration of being naked outside. Until now we've only ever had sex here once – that first time. Sneaking in after hours to drink champagne and fool around had seemed daring enough to me. But Charles wanted to make tonight extra special.

He fastens a long chain to my collar and gently tugs me to follow him. The shackles are heavy but they don't hinder me that much, at least not as long as I am on all fours. Waves of heat and desire wash over me as he guides me towards the black iron portcullis. When we reach it he urges me up and I get shakily to my feet. My legs barely feel capable of supporting me but somehow I manage to stand.

Charles loops the long chain through the latticework of the portcullis and locks it in place. I can move perhaps a couple of feet in either direction but I'm firmly tethered to the gate. Next he attaches a clip to the chain between my wrists and hoists my arms up over my head, fixing them to a higher point on the grille. The position forces me up on my toes. I pull gently at my bonds, just enough to confirm how helpless I am, and the chains jingle like laughter at my plight. I hear Charles moving away and

I take several deep breaths to calm my galloping heart.

I am filled with fear. Fear of the pain, the helplessness, the danger of exposure. What if I scream and someone hears me and calls the police? What if I can't take it and I break down, sobbing like a child? What if I disappoint him? What if, what if?

When he is standing beside me again I detect the scent of leather and my breath catches in my throat. He doesn't say a word. He doesn't have to. He runs a single finger down the line of my spine and I shudder in anticipation. His stillness calms me, reminding me to be brave, to make him proud. I wrap my fingers around the bars of the iron grille, arching my back for him. This is the point of no return, the point at which I prepare myself to take whatever he wants to give me.

He moves away again and I turn my head just enough to see him running his fingers through the tails of a long leather whip. The tresses fan out as they fall, swinging heavily from his hand. I swallow my fear and face the portcullis. Then I hear the tails cut through the air.

The lashes slap against my bare back and I yelp, mostly out of surprise. It's not as painful as I'd feared. I relax a little as he plays the whip over my back, making me jump and yelp. But it's bearable. Even strangely calming.

My skin begins to tingle with warmth and I squirm a little as I grow wetter. I lean forward into the gate, pushing my bottom out for him. He doesn't neglect any part of me. The lashes fall gently across my cheeks and down my thighs, then back up across my shoulders. The tails lick round my chest, flicking my breasts. I gasp each time the leather kisses my nipples, my arse, my sex. All the places that belong to him.

The rhythm slows and the strokes become lighter, as though he is gradually inching away as he whips me. By now I am nearly in a trance from the stimulation and I'm craving more. He stops long enough to let me savour the prickly heat and the musky scent of leather. Then he begins again in earnest.

This time the lashes bite deep, making me jump and twist in my bonds. The chains jangle against the iron grille and I cry out in pain, straining away from the whip. But I can't get away. Again and again the fierce leather slices down across my back, setting my tender skin on fire. I always tell myself I'll take it with grace and dignity but it's precisely that grace and dignity Charles so loves breaking down.

He takes his time, sometimes waiting several seconds between strokes, letting the pain from the last one build and consume me and fade before giving me the next one. I press my mouth against my arm and bite down to stifle my cry at a particularly hard stroke. The dense heat swarms over my already burning flesh, devouring it. And even though the pain is considerable, my body responds with pleasure. My sex pulses and throbs in response and I long to rub my thighs together.

A flurry of gentle strokes follow, the lashes softly flicking around to catch my breasts again. The tails sting my tender nipples and when the whip moves away I press them against the chill of the iron gate, gasping at the cold.

He brings the whip down across my back again with force and again I stifle my scream. My flesh burns and throbs and my eyes fill with tears, turning the portcullis into an underwater blur. The pain builds and subsides, builds and subsides, and I am carried away on its waves, lost in the delirious zone where it shades into pleasure and I can no longer tell the difference between the two.

The whip slaps softly against my inner thighs and I obey its wordless instruction, parting my legs as much as the shackles will allow. Charles aims a series of light strokes up against my sex. The leather tresses smack against my swollen wetness, sending jolts of ecstasy through me. My thighs strain with the effort of holding me up and I will myself not to come until I am given permission. I hope he won't make me wait too long.

But after each taste of pleasure comes another taste of pain. The lashes slice against my back again, making me writhe and cry out. The chains rattle Chaie leather and I clutch the grille, hissing through my teeth until the intensity begins to fade. Again and again he repeats the pattern: a gentle stroke, then a harsh one. I'm gripping the iron bars so tightly I feel welded to it. Another sensual flick of the leather tails against my sex, another vicious slash across my upper back, then another, then another.

Lights flash behind my eyes and suddenly I no longer feel the pain. It's as though I've left it – and my body – behind. I let go of the grille, my arms hanging limply in my shackles as my head buzzes with endorphins and my sex pulses with need.

I feel weightless, as though the chains are the only things keeping me from floating away, drifting up into the sky. Time seems to slow and the stars above me are a golden smear of light. I can still taste the champagne and I smile as I imagine that I'm trapped inside its tiny bubbles, light and effervescent. I could dissolve into a million particles of ecstasy. My heart throbs in my chest like the beat of a tribal drum, an ancient rhythm that slowly, slowly brings me back down to earth. The whip seems to fall in time with its thumping; grounding me, returning me.

The strokes grow lighter and fainter, as Charles eases me out of the moment. Nothing exists in the world except the two of us. I whimper softly, entreating and thanking him.

'Good girl,' he whispers in my ear. 'Such a good girl.'

I lean my head back and he kisses away the tears on my face. His hands cup my breasts from behind, his warm touch intensifying both the stinging pain and the pleasure. I feel his hardness press against my tender arse and then his fingers travel down along my sides and across my abdomen, down at last to my eager pussy.

He slides his fingers along the dewy slit, making me gasp. Each teasing brush of his fingers against my clit wrenches another pleading little cry from me until he must know I can't take any more.

'I'm going to make you come now,' he says, 'and then I'm going to fuck you.'

A grateful little whimper is all I can manage.

He slips a finger inside me from behind, then another. With his other hand he gently strokes my clit. He presses his finger against the swollen little bud and slides it back and forth. Each touch is electric. He increases the friction, rubbing me faster and harder. My body jumps in response to each little surge of pleasure, building and building until it breaks over me in a flood. He continues swirling his fingers inside me, manipulating my G-spot to prolong the climax. It feels like it will never stop. And when the aftershock at last begins to fade I am left gasping and panting and utterly devastated.

After a while his hands move away and then I feel his cock between my legs. I haven't even noticed him removing his trousers. He buries himself in me easily and begins to fuck me. Short controlled thrusts, then long languid strokes. Each time he plunges himself in I am reminded of the vicious slashes of the whip. His skin against mine reawakens both the pain and pleasure and the chains rattle against the grille with the force of his thrusts.

'My beautiful little slave,' he murmurs in my ear, 'such a good girl for her master.'

The words excite me as much as his cock. I moan in response, rolling my hips and clenching myself around him to heighten his pleasure. The cold friction of the grille is almost unbearably stimulating against my nipples and I lean back into him so his hands can reach my breasts. He squeezes them, each one just more than a handful, and my nipples burn with comforting warmth.

His cock fills me again and again and sudd Cgaitinueenly, impossibly, I feel the twinges of another orgasm. It mounts with his increased passion and my body bucks and leaps like a horse's against him as he holds me tighter, emptying himself into me in short hot bursts.

I have no idea how long we stay there, pressed tightly together, drifting and basking. But at some point Charles slips away and the world gradually begins to reform around me. I hear the distant clink of chains and it's some time before I realise he's unlocked the shackles. I collapse into his arms and he carries me back to where my clothes are, back to where mundane reality waits to claim us. An owl twitters nearby, a sound so familiar and commonplace that it fills my eyes with tears. I don't want to leave, don't want to go back to the real world. I want to stay in the bubble of ecstasy forever.

Sensing my distress, Charles enfolds me in his arms. I cling to him, crying from the intensity of the experience.

Thrill Seekers

I'm so disorientated. It's as if my mind doesn't know how to process the whole powerful cocktail of pleasure, pain and total surrender. None of our games have ever reduced me to such a profound level of submission before.

'I'm happy,' I manage to choke out, wanting to reassure him even in my confusion. 'I'm so happy. And I love you so much. So I don't know why I'm crying. I'm sorry.'

He smiles down at me and his expression tells me he understands everything. 'Amy,' he says, stroking my face and wiping away my tears, 'you don't ever have to go back.'

I blink in confusion, sniffling. 'What do you mean?'

He puts the shackles back into the holdall. Then he carefully coils the whip and lays it on top of the chains. He touches my throat and I realise he hasn't removed the collar. Its comforting weight infuses me with sudden warmth.

His eyes are blue-black in the glint of the moonlight. 'You belong to me,' he says. 'Forever. As my wife and my slave. Happy anniversary, darling.'

I blush and lower my head, suddenly feeling foolish. He'd only hinted at such permanence before in fantasy but we never actually discussed it. Now I saw that there had never been any need. Charles knew me better than I knew myself. He'd known me from the moment we met in this very spot all those years ago.

And as I knelt at his feet and let him dress me for the ride home, I gazed over at the portcullis and wondered what next year's visit would bring.

Making It Work
Tenille Brown

It was all Dig's bright idea.

The video, not the sex. Retha had always been fine with the sex, even with all the new and inventive things her husband had wanted to try lately.

The man always had something up his sleeves these days. Retha considered it the male equivalent to empty nest syndrome. It seemed he had been running buck naked through the house since their daughter, Candace, had left, and that was three years ago.

It got worse when Candace up and decided to get married, though. Dig knew for sure then that their little girl wasn't coming back.

So, he filled the time and space with his ideas.

Like the handcuffs and the nipple clamps. The dildos and anal beads.

So, of course, the presence of the camera shouldn't have

been surprising to her at all. But why Dig decided that now was the time to film their escapades was beyond her.

Retha had agreed, though. After all, she had become a little restless, too.

She wasn't working as much as she used to down at the car dealership where Dig was a manager. Her friends were caught up in their own little things these days, like grandkids and retirement.

Retha didn't have either of those things going for her, not yet. All she had was Dig and the house. Or, more specifically, Dig chasing her around the house trying to fuck her in the strangest ways in the strangest places.

As had become the norm with Dig, it couldn't be as simple as setting up a camcorder on a tripod and hopping in the bed.

No, this evening there were props and outfits, tools and ticklers, enough for three nights of sex all combined into their one-night naked documentary.

But like a good little wife, Retha was waiting for Dig as he had requested, sprawled across the bed in a faux leather corset and matching thong on her voluptuous size twelve body.

Master/slave was the theme tonight, he had been sure to point that out, and Retha had been sure to meet the requirements.

Retha heard keys in the door and positioned herself accordingly on the bed, in perfect angle in front of the camera. She didn't know how long she could hold the position, and she imagined Dig would take his time getting up the stairs, as dramatic as he was about everything bedroom-related these days.

The front door opened, and there were footsteps on the hardwood floor. But when Retha listened closely, it wasn't Dig's voice that she heard. It was much softer, lighter. It was feminine.

It was her sister, Diane.

There was no time to curse and verbally regret ever giving her a spare key no matter how good an idea it seemed at the time. Right now there were bigger things to worry about, like getting off the bed before Diane barged in, like covering up in something decent before Retha gave poor Diane a heart attack.

Retha was up off the bed in a flash. She grabbed her terry cloth robe from the back of the door and threw it on, tying the sash tightly around her waist.

Not only had Diane let herself in, she was making her way up the stairs.

She couldn't let Diane see the bedroom like this. Retha threw the whip in a corner and covered it up with a pair of Dig's pants. Then there was the video camera, there would be no time to take it down.

Diane was coming. She had almost reached the top step. 'Retha are you up here? Did I wake you?'

Retha heard Diane's hand on the doorknob, so she

sprinted to it and pulled it open just enough that she could wedge her own way out.

'Diane!' She forced the excitement in her voice. 'What a surprise. I was just getting in the shower.'

Then Diane looked down. And so did Retha, at her fishnet-covered legs.

'Um ... I see ...' Diane stammered.

But Retha didn't have to worry about explaining any further. They were both interrupted by another entry in the front door, and Dig's booming voice travelling up the stairs where they both stood, awkward and silent.

'Retha, big daddy's ho–'

Dig stopped short, his eyes darting back and forth between the two women.

Retha knew the scenario would have been funny if she wasn't already so annoyed. But to see the look on Dig's face was still enough to make her chuc Kmak wokle just a little.

She interjected before Dig could say anything.

'Dig, Diane decided to pop in for a few days. Isn't that right, Diane?'

'Yes, it is,' Diane said. 'And I'm sorry I didn't give any notice, but it was a rush decision, very last minute, really so ...'

But Retha didn't think Dig was listening. She could see the light fading in his eyes, his childlike excitement slowly vanishing.

Retha hoped like hell he hadn't already taken his Viagra.

'Anytime,' Dig said. 'You know you're welcome in our home anytime at all, Diane.'

But surely you would have thought he had a vacuum connected to him, the way the life seemed to be sucked right out of him.

* * *

Retha waited until they were alone later in the evening to cut to the chase.

'So, what brings you here, Diane? And I don't want to hear that "checking up on me" bullshit, either. You left Don home and you haven't even mentioned him. So, you tell me right now what's going on,' Retha demanded.

And just like that, Diane sprung a leak.

She collapsed over the kitchen counter in a heap, her bony shoulders shaking as she sobbed.

'It's over, Retha,' she said. 'I'm leaving him.'

Crap, Retha thought. Now we'll never fuck again.

But what Retha said was, 'Why on earth would you do that, Diane? You guys just celebrated an anniversary. Your what … thirteenth?'

'Yeah, well, what the hell does that mean when you've got a hot little number doing the things you used to want your wife to do?'

Retha exhaled and mentally counted to ten.

'So, you're saying he's cheating,' she said.

'He has to be,' Diane said between wails and sobs.

'So, you don't know this for sure.' Retha was looking at her hysterical sister and rubbing her on the shoulder, trying to calm her.

'Well, we're not … you know … at all any more … so if he's not … *doing* me … then who is he … *doing*?'

Diane had a point, but Retha didn't want to say as much. If she wanted her house and her sex life back, she had to stay on the positive side of things like somehow getting Diane out of there and back home to her husband.

'It's going to be fine, Diane, and I promise we'll get to the bottom of this, but for now you just settle in and you can stay as long as you need to.'

Diane could only manage a nod before she started crying hysterically again and Retha wondered just what she had gotten herself into.

* * *

It was hard to enjoy Dig's hands through Diane's sniffling, but Retha sure tried, leaning into her burly husband as he slid his arm behind her, slipping his large hand into the waistband of her stretchy pants.

He was gently massaging her round ass over her panties.

Retha was smiling at the television screen, though she

couldn't have repeated to anyone what might have been happening in the movie.

She was concentrating on she and Dig's own little private show, getting their tenderness in where they could.

Since her sister had been there, it was hard to get their little escapades in at night. They had tried at first, pretending everything was as normal. But it was hard to feel sexy with Diane in the next room, crying half the night. Even Dig couldn't block it out long enough to make it happen. And Diane was always at the house, always. Cooking, cleaning. Earning her keep, she said.

The crying was worse when Diane tried to control it, the sniffles became snorts and her shoulders shook in mini spasms as she blew her nose into a wad of tissue.

Frustrated, Retha nudged Dig's hand away and sat straight up on the couch.

'Why did you even want to watch the damned movie, Diane?' she asked her sister, frustrated now.

Diane looked at her, her eyes glossy, her cheeks flushed.

'I'm sorry, but I didn't know it would do this ... to me!'

And Diane sprang from the sofa and ran up the stairs, the door to the guest bedroom slamming shut behind her.

Retha shook her head and turned the television off.

Dig was leaning in, seemingly oblivious to the scene that had just played out in their living room.

His lips were on Retha's, and he was groping her breasts through her cashmere sweater like a horny teenager.

'We can't possible do this now,' Retha said. 'And certainly not here. Diane has just managed to kill the mood yet again.'

'She's been killing the mood since she's been here,' Dig said and Retha couldn't help but nod in agreement.

She missed her husband. The laying beside him every night, feeling him harden behind her in the wee hours of the morning was torture.

It had been nearly a week. Six, long and awful days of lying beside each other in pyjamas instead of in the nude because they never knew when tactless Diane might barge in wanting to talk.

They showered with the door closed, they didn't even have playtime in the shower because they didn't want to make her feel bad, rubbing their rambunctious sex life in her face when she was certain her marriage was over.

'Let's just go on up to bed,' Retha said, patting Dig on his thigh.

'Yes, to bed. The highlight of my evening.'

Dig didn't mask his sarcasm, and Retha didn't acknowledge it. Instead she followed her husband up the stairs, thinking of which modest nightgown she would wear tonight as they lay beside each other as if there were an invisible line drawn between them.

* * *

It was worth a shot.

Diane was in the den reading the paper. She had gone two consecutive hours without crying. Retha had been timing her. She figured maybe the woman had finally run her well bone dry.

Retha waited in the cramped quarters of their outside pantry until she finally heard Dig's footsteps as he was passing by. He was on his way to take out the trash when Retha opened the pantry door and pulled him in, the bag of trash falling from his hand.

She closed the door once he was inside. It was dark but for the candle she had lit and placed on a high shelf.

'What the hell ...' Dig looked around him.

They barely even used this place. It was cold and it was dusty and it was outdoors for heaven's sake, but Retha had decided they would make use of it this evening.

Kevewidth="

Retha shushed him by covering his moustached lips with her own.

She stopped kissing him long enough to say, 'Diane's reading the paper, and after that she'll go upstairs for her shower. She's a creature of habit. That woman never changes a thing. Now, I say that gives us ten minutes at least, maybe twelve. You think you can find anything interesting to do with the time?'

She pressed her body against him, in case he needed convincing.

Dig whispered, 'We still have time to make it to the bedroom, don't we?'

Retha began unfastening Dig's jeans as she responded. 'Why waste the time going up the stairs when right here is just fine?'

She was kissing her husband's neck between words, her lips travelling down the front of his body.

Retha lowered herself until she was on her knees, taking Dig's cock inside her hands. Dig breathed what seemed like a sigh of relief and leaned back against an empty shelf.

He parted his legs so that Retha could wedge herself comfortably there, mouth level with his hard and ready cock.

At last, Retha took Dig in her mouth.

The weight of his stiffened cock was heavy on her tongue. She brought her mouth down the length of it, running her tongue along the top and sides. She gently sucked and teasingly lapped at it, her eyes closed, her fingers massaging Dig's taut little ass and strong, hairy thighs.

The outside pantry certainly wasn't their king-sized bed, but it would do. There were no bells and whistles out here, no video cameras and such, but Retha had to admit, the limited space and she giving Dig the best head of his life was rather exciting.

Retha released his cock, only to take his scrotum into

her mouth. His balls bounced with the motion of her tongue. She felt Dig begin to quiver, and she knew it wasn't from the cold.

'I won't last long, this way,' Dig said, and Retha knew as much, but she continued on as if he hadn't said anything at all, alternating with her mouth between his cock and his scrotum.

And no, at this rate, they wouldn't have time to get to her, but that was fine, too. Pleasing Dig with her tongue was giving Retha a new and exciting sensation all its own. She felt she could climax from just the thought and the rush alone, but there wouldn't be time.

Dig grabbed a handful of Retha's thick, curly hair.

She loved when her man got rough with her. She wanted him to pull at it harder, but she didn't want to stop long enough to tell him, so she let out a little moan to encourage him.

Dig got the hint. He jerked her head back so fiercely that she almost lost balance and her mouth's grip on his cock.

She regained her balance, though, there on her knees and continued her oral gift to him.

'Fuck,' Dig said. 'I'm coming.'

Retha gripped harder with her lips and with her jaws. She continued to pull as Dig released his seed inside her cheeks.

She swallowed.

She smiled.

Then Retha said, 'Let's go back inside before Diane comes looking for us.'

She got up and dusted off the knees of her jeans. Then she left Dig alone in the outside pantry to dress and regain his composure.

* * *

Retha never thought she her Kughdivd see the day when she wouldn't be able to get properly laid in her own damned house. She was outside trimming the shrubs as she thought about it. She wasn't one for yard work, but it was something to keep her hands busy, because lord knows since that night in the pantry, they hadn't been busy doing anything else, like holding onto Dig's cock, or guiding it toward her waiting sex.

She couldn't even masturbate properly. She had tried that this morning after Dig had gone to work and she thought Diane had laid back down for a nap.

But, five minutes in, who had come knocking on the bathroom door looking for the shampoo? Damn Diane.

Retha halted when she realised that she was all but butchering her shrubs. Her fingers ached inside the thick gloves and she was pouring sweat in one of Dig's flannel shirts.

She put the trimmers down and noticed that she had been outside so long the sun was beginning to set.

When Dig's truck drove up, she cracked half a smile and waved him over.

He kissed her on her moist forehead and Retha could hardly take it. It had been nine days now and even the feel of his lips on the most innocent of places weakened her knees.

'Where is she?' he asked.

She was Diane, of course, and that question was always the conversation opener these days.

Retha nodded toward the house. 'She's inside making dinner. She said it was the least she could do since she was *imposing*.'

'The least she could do?' Dig repeated. Then he shook his head.

'I'm sorry,' Retha said, apologising for what felt like the hundredth time since Diane had been there.

'You don't have to apologise. She's your sister and you're doing the right thing. It's no big deal. We have the rest of our lives.'

'Well, it feels like we'll die first,' Retha said, her head down, shoulders sagging.

Dig squinted at Retha in the fading sunlight. 'Now, I wouldn't want that to happen.'

Dig grabbed Retha by the waist and pulled her to him. He kissed her hard, encouraging her mouth open with his tongue. She was going limp in his arms, she could feel it. And at this rate, if he kept doing what he was doing with that thing, he would have to drag her dead weight inside the house and lay her down on the couch.

'Dig, you have … to stop that …' she managed to say.

Dig paused to look her directly in the eyes. 'You sure you want me to stop?' he asked, continuing to run his hands along the side of her body, 'because all the signs are pointing to no.'

'But, you know we can't … all we're doing is torturing ourselves, and in front of the neighbourhood!'

Dig kissed her some more. 'Maybe not. All we need is a little time, and a little place.'

This time it was Retha who pulled back and looked at Dig.

'I don't know if we can squeeze in that pantry again, Dig. It was hell on my back and knees last time, she said.

'No, I was thinking of someplace else,' Dig said.

He took his wife by the hand and led her to the back of the house. It was getting darker by the minute.

Autumn leaves crunched beneath their feet as they made their way to what Retha soon realised was their storage shed.

'Here?' Retha asked, her concern o Kherlign="justbvious in her expression.

'I was thinking more like behind the shed,' Dig said, and led her there by the hand.

Standing there, Dig stripped Retha of his flannel shirt and laid it there on the cool earth.

'Wouldn't want that pretty ass getting cold,' he said.

Retha was standing there in a T-shirt and old jeans now, so stunned she didn't know what to do next. But Dig helped her with the rest of her clothes as well, at least, the bottom half.

He eased her out of her jeans and her lacy panties. He left the T-shirt on.

'Like old times,' he whispered in her ear. 'When you used to fuck me like you were shy. Didn't want to show your tits. Scared to show your whole body.'

'But you've seen it all since then,' Retha said between applying kisses to Dig's neck. 'You know exactly what's going on under there.'

'Yes, I do,' Dig agreed, squeezing one breast through the cotton of her white T-shirt.

He eased his wife onto the ground, lying on top of her.

Dig only shed his pants and boxers, as well, leaving on his pale-blue button-down shirt.

'I don't know what kind of time we're working with before our house guest comes a calling, but, baby, I'm determined to make the most of it.

Dig placed Retha's hand on his cock.

'You feel that?'

Retha nodded.

'That's over a week of watching you wiggle and prance around this house and not being able to lay a hand on you.'

He let it rest between Retha's thighs for a minute. She reached down and began to massage it.

'Damn, I've missed you. I never thought I'd say that to the man who sleeps beside me every night.' Retha's breathing was hurried.

'I like hearing it," Dig said.

He nibbled on Retha's ear, and eased his fingers through her hair. He couldn't wait any longer. He had to be inside her, at least for a little while.

Dig eased his cock inside's Retha's opening. She immediately clung to him, latching on as he pushed further, then pulled back, his rhythmic motion encouraging unintelligible sounds from her mouth.

The ground was cold, hard and rough against her back, but Retha didn't care. She pulled on Dig's hips, begging him to move faster and to press harder.

Twigs snapped beneath them. She heard a squirrel scurry in the woods.

Retha wrapped her legs around Dig's waist. She was lying her head all the way down now, fuck getting dirt and leaves in her hair, damn having to explain it all to Diane once they were back inside.

Dig was her husband and she needed his cock, and she needed it now.

'Fuck, give it to me!' Retha growled.

She adjusted herself so that she was on all fours. She knew this would make him weak. She knew he would barely be able to brace himself on his knees for long when he was entering her from the back. The sensation would set him ablaze, and he would be climaxing within minutes.

But that was all right, because Retha's was already on the way.

She felt it at the base of her belly.

She was getting wetter, Dig was holding on tighter to her waist as he slid in and out of her.

'Not yet,' he said, begging. 'Not yet. I want you to wait for me.'

But Retha couldn't wait. Her legs were shaking and the muscles in her abdomen were tightening.

She knew what was next.

'I'm coming,' she said to Dig between his pelvic thrusts and her biting down on her lips.

'That's OK, too,' Dig said, increasing the rate of his pumping.

He was pulling at her T-shirt now and Retha could hear it ripping and, for fuck's sake, this excited her more. Dig pulled until the T-shirt tore off her body.

If it was a cold night, Retha didn't notice. All she knew was that she was hot, hot for Dig, hot for this.

Even after a spine-tingling orgasm, Dig had revved her up again, and could it be, she would come twice before her husband even came once?

Yes, it was absolutely true. Retha felt it coming on strong.

'I'm coming again,' Retha gasped, grabbing up a piece of her torn shirt. She placed it between her teeth and bit down on the soft cotton.

She used it to muffle her scream because she knew she would really let loose this time.

And she did. She screamed as hard as she came, and this fuelled Dig's own climax which he spewed furiously inside her.

They stayed that way, still, for a few minutes, catching their breath, fondling each other's bodies. Who knew when the opportunity would present itself again?

'You go in first,' Retha said, 'and distract her. I'll sneak in through the side, seeing as how I'm topless and all.'

They both giggled into the night.

Dig stood up on his feet. And Retha watched as he was slow and careful about putting on his boxers and pants.

'We've got to stop meeting like this,' he said and winked.

Retha stood next and smacked him playfully on the ass, winking right back at him.

* * *

When Retha and Diane came in from buying groceries, Dig was on the phone.

'I understand, man. I went through the same thing

Erotic Encounters

myself a couple of years ago. Went to my family doctor, told him the deal, and got myself fixed right up.'

Dig nodded in response to whatever whoever it was on the phone was telling him.

'I'm telling you. It's just as simple as that.'

Dig nodded some more. Then he asked, 'Well, wouldn't you like to tell that to your wife?'

Retha looked at Diane and Diane looked at Dig.

Dig said, 'Diane, enough is enough. Don wants to speak to you.'

* * *

Yes, it had really been that simple. As simple as Don admitting to Diane that he'd had problems getting it up and was embarrassed by it. No, there was no other woman. No, he hadn't lost interest in her.

Diane was on the next flight out.

Retha and Dig had their place back, and sure enough, in Dig's fashion, he had the camera set up in their bedroom that very night.

He was wearing leather chaps, his still fine and firm brown ass showing, teasing her.

'Are you ready for your big film debut?' he asked playfully, watching his leather-clad wife s Kr-cIprawled and spread-eagled across the bed.

'Absolutely,' Retha said. 'But I was thinking, you don't

138

see a lot of nature films lately. Maybe we can do something, set ... I don't know ... outside somewhere?'

'Good thinking, lady,' Dig said. 'You grab a blanket. I'll disassemble this damned thing.'

...was lucky in... this study. Naughty as I dreamt
that... I don't know... I just can't wait for the
Church darkens. Later, Dr. said 'Sis, you will enjoy
I'll answer the this human thing.

Park and Ride
Victoria Blisse

I sit in the park after dark. I'm not scared. I know how to defend myself if trouble does come my way, but the teens they keep to themselves in the dark corner by the bowling green. I sit on a bench by the rose garden, the heady scent heavy in the air around me. It's fresh and musky and smells of seduction and lust. I sit and wait, not for anyone in particular, just someone.

It is not a fact that is widely published, I've not even heard it whispered in dark corners in disreputable bars at night, but a certain kind of person knows that the park is the place to be after nightfall if you want a certain kind of illicit thrill, the kind that will get you arrested if you're not careful. But the police do a sweep of the place once at eleven o'clock. Sometimes they'll move the teens on if they're being rowdy but mostly they drive through and tick it off their to-do list. The people I am looking for come out later.

Sometimes they smell of beer, they've come to finish off a good night out, other times the only thing you can sense is loneliness. I'm not either of those. I'm not drunk and I'm not desperate. I just want to fuck. Yeah, people think I'm a freak. I have a pink streak through my hair, a few more piercings than most are comfortable with and I wear what I like, fashion and propriety be damned. I have no trouble picking up boys the old-fashioned way but I'm not interested in that. I don't want a boyfriend, I just want sex. Hot, animalistic sex in the dark. In the park. I am addicted to the risk.

I'm early, it's only just gone midnight; the park is empty of human life but buzzing with sound. The light breeze rustles in the trees, bushes scuffle; if you're lucky you glimpse a fox or a cat or a rat as they go about their nightly business. The sound of the road carries mutely through, not many cars pass so late but the sound of engines, voices and high heels carry across the night sky at irregular intervals. I enjoy the cool of the summer's evening after the oppressive heat of the day. My skin tingles with the combination of cool air and sexual anticipation. I've never had a disappointing visit to the park, not after hours anyway.

A shadowy figure comes in through the gates and looks furtively left and right. A good sign, there's no dog beside him and he's looking for something. I can tell it's a man by the way he strides and as the glare of the streetlight behind him fades I can see more of his outline. Tall, thin, striding purposefully. I shift on the bench, eager energy flowing through me. I lean forward a bit more, showing off the low cleavage of my top. I don't want to mess about.

'Hi.' His voice is deep and commanding, I like that. 'Do you mind if I sit with you?'

'No, go ahead. It's a beautiful evening.' I'm pretty certain we're both here for the same thing but it is a duel, a dance, a game. I'd be disappointed if he didn't play it.

'It is. Look, this is going to sound corny, but don't I know you?'

I turn to look, my heart beating out of my chest. Have I been discovered?

'I don't know cipa Nok,' I take in his features. A hard chin, wide eyes, soft lips and just the tiniest glimmer of recognition. I'm relieved he definitely isn't a workmate or a friend of mum's from church or someone who'd be really pissed off, thank God. '… you do seem familiar.'

'I shouldn't ask,' he whispers, staring hard at me in the gloom, 'but what's your name?'

By this point I'm usually engaged in heavy petting at the very least. This guy wants my name?

'Carrie.'

So why the hell did I give it to him?

'Oh, fuck, it is you! I'm Grant. I sat behind you in maths at Our Ladies comp, geez, small world.'

142

'Holy crap, Grant! Well, this is a bit awkward.' My cheeks flush with heat. The game is up!

'Why, aren't you here for sex?' His eyebrow quirks and I wonder if the night might just be salvageable.

'That is exactly why I'm here, but do you want to fuck me?' The question hangs on the air, wrapped in rose musk and heavy with intent.

'Yes,' he whispers and leans forward until our lips meet. I press eagerly back, the excitement pumping through my veins. I've always kissed strangers in the dark but never felt the same buzz as explodes between Grant and me. I grab him, run my hands over his chest and ruffle up handfuls of his soft T-shirt. He growls and pulls me tighter to him; the sound vibrates through my lips, the roughness of his action echoes through my body. I am more than ready to fuck him.

It wasn't like we ever talked much at school. I was a weirdo freak and he was just a geek. He helped me a couple of times when I was completely befuddled by some new mathematical torture, but apart from admiring the startling bright blue of his eyes I didn't pay him any attention. If I'd know he was this good at kissing I'd have been all over him.

'Like a fucking dream come true,' he mumbles, lips slipping down my neck, nibbling on erogenous zones and making me purr, 'I always wanted to do this.' He cups my breasts and dips his kisses into the low cleavage of my top. I reach around him and trace my fingers up his back, below his top to encourage him. He lifts one boob and then the other from my bra. They pull wide the 'V' of my T-shirt and dangle enticingly over the cups of my bra. The cool air tickles them, my nipples crinkle further and the tightening makes me gasp with desire. He looks for a moment then continues to kiss and lick, nibble and suck until I am a complete mess of lust. I wonder if Grant has a girlfriend at home, I wonder if it is his first trip here after dark. I wonder about his cock. I am all over the place, boiling over with need.

Running my fingers around his waist I fumble to undo his belt, button and zipper. I feel the heat and the movement inside and am thrilled to find him without underwear. He's obviously come for a good time. His cock is hot, hard and I want it. He keeps feasting on my breasts as I coax his erection out of his trousers and stroke it. He's long, thick and softly strong. I love that paradox, the rigidity and softness of a man's aroused dick is something that keeps me eager to sample more. One of life's sweetest conundrums.

'Fuck me,' I groan, 'Grant, fuck me.' I can't wait any more, I need him now. He looks up, even in the murk I can see the darker flush to his cheeks and his eyes sparkle with mischief.

'Yes.' He looks round eager to find the perfect place for us to fuck. I could give him a few pointers, though

I'm not going to lie back on the bench again. No, the last time I did that I had to get a mate of mine to pick out the splin Soutones anters in my back for me the next day. Ouch! Although the prickle and stab of the rough wood the night before had triggered off an almighty orgasm, so I suppose that made up for the pain and the embarrassment. As he thinks, I slip to my knees on the broken up, old tarmac. The grit digs into my exposed knees, my short skirt finishing a couple of inches higher so providing no protection, but I don't care, I want to taste him. I trace my fingers around him, getting my bearings in the dark. His moan cuts through the dark hum of night and I follow the path of my fingers with my tongue. I press my body between his thighs, stretch my neck and lap at his cock. He smells and tastes of citrus ice cream, mellow and sweet but with a zing that is refreshing and addictive. I lap around the tip of his erection, his juices are delicious and I love knowing that I turn him on that much.

I slide my mouth around him and he stiffens. I wonder if he's heard someone approach so I stop in my tracks. His whimper lets me know all is fine and I continue to drop lower before rising up again and kissing his tip. He clasps the back of my head in his hand, interlacing my hair in his fingers. He gently encourages me to take more of him with every sweep of my mouth. My hands are resting on his inner thighs; I move the right hand up to stroke at his balls. They wrinkle in delight. I really want to taste him, feel the power of making him come with just my lips and the odd stroking finger but I also really need to be fucked. I pull my head away from his erection with a *pop*. I wink and scramble over the tarmac and into the lush grass by the roses. I look back, wiggle my arse and giggle. Thankfully Grant gets the message.

He shuffles over, holding his trousers up with one hand then drops them and himself to the grass behind me.

'You've got protection, right?' I ask before things go too far. I may like sex in risky places but I'm not stupid enough to play those kinds of games.

'Yeah, don't worry,' he replies and slaps my arse play-fully. I moan and wiggle encouragingly. I won't be able to get a thorough spanking here, in public, but encouraging a few further spanks will certainly spice up the encounter. I love the heat and the pain and the heightened pleasure of a firm hand smacking down on my bum.

'Oh, you like that, huh? Kinky bitch.' He slaps me again, a little harder and the moan that squeaks through my squeezed lips sounds like a whimper. I like to be dominated. I would never have marked Grant down as one to take control. Just goes to show, you can't judge a geek by his cover. Or something like that. I'm too turned on to complete metaphors correctly, or recognise what one of them actually is.

Grant pushes himself up against my bum and leans

over my back. I can feel his cock digging into me through the material of my skirt. The fucking tease is driving me wild. I want him inside me and I want it now.

'Someone's watching,' he hisses. 'Should we stop?'

I look to my left, see nothing but rose bushes then look to my right. There is a figure kneeling down behind a clump of roses maybe ten feet away or so.

'It's OK,' I reply, grinding myself against his crotch, 'I think it's just Joe. He likes to watch.'

Joe isn't his real name, we've never spoken. It's just what I call him. He's seen me fuck here a few times. I've never seen him get it on with anyone. He just watches and wanks. That must be his thing.

'Well, if you're sure –'

'I am sure. Now fuck me,' I demand. My fuse is short, I want to come. I don't want to mess about any more.

' S"ju ItI'm the boss,' he growls and slaps my arse again, 'I'll fuck you when I'm good and ready.'

I know you can't come from words alone but I am pretty close to exploding. I told you I love to be dominated. Grant flicks up my skirt and runs a hand over my naked buttocks.

'No knickers, I should have known. You've always been a naughty girl.' He runs a thick finger down the crack between my soft orbs, over my clenching anus and lower into my damp folds. He presses forward and enters me, see-sawing in and out. Wet squelches ring out as he delves deeper into me, the slurping sound is crude and raw.

'You're so fucking wet, slut,' he exclaims, driving more fingers into me, stretching me, playing with me. 'You love this, don't you?'

I'm lost in sensations, my knees sinking into the mud, grinding out the grass scent, his fingers inside me, the cold breeze on my exposed arse. It's not until he reaches forward and grasps my hair that I realise he's asked a question.

'You love it, don't you?' Grant asks again, holding my head back with one hand, filling my pussy with fingers of the other.

'Yes, yes, I do,' I reply, my scalp stinging, my pussy contracting around his digits.

'That's better.' He lets go of my hair and strokes my back. I imagine it is to soothe me but I am aroused all the further. When will he fuck me? I hear rustling leaves and look up, it's just Joe. He must be growing restless too.

I feel empty when he pulls his fingers from inside me. He slaps me with them; I can feel how wet they are. The imprint of my juices chills his handprint into my buttock. I am marked by my own wantonness. I am exposed and waiting. A crinkling noise adds to the low hum of the night as Grant unwraps a condom and puts it on. The darkness seems to cradle me, the whip of the wind like a lover's caress makes me shiver with delight. My sex is wide open and exposed, lewdly displayed right there in a public place but the embrace of night makes it OK, keeps my desires secreted away from those who wouldn't approve. It wraps me, Grant and our watcher in a thin veil of security, but I am on my guard, anyway. My heart hammers with want but also with a little fear.

I start when he touches my thigh, a sign of how on edge I feel.

'Are you OK?' Grant asks and I smile. It's good to be cared for.

'Yes,' I reply. 'Fuck me, please.'

I am starting to become cold and uncomfortable on all fours in the grass, the moistness coats my hands and knees, chilling me. I feel as if I'm sinking deeper into the mud below the grass. Will there be dents here tomorrow?

Grant doesn't wait around and slots himself and his stiff erection between my thighs. He presses closer to me and I wriggle to help line him up with my aching, damp pussy. He fills me and I clamp my lips against a cry of absolute delight. This is what I want, the ache inside me is relieved by his cock sliding into me. I stretch around him then squeeze him tight and I feel good. When he fills me completely a new ache begins and I pull forward, wanting him to move. I hear Joe gasp and I'm reminded of his presence. Having this intimate moment witnessed makes it more exciting, lifts a simple sex act to the level of a kink. And I like being kinky. I love it.

I am sure fucking in a big soft bed with candles and rose petals must be very pleasurable, but I prefer dirty, down in the flowerbed sex. Grant groans and grunts, shunts his hips forward and slides them back, the pace quickens and I lose myself in the cacophony of lust that races through my body. My eyelids dro Sy emplep instinctively to keep me from falling apart but I force them wide, I want to remember every detail, I want to experience it all. The shadowy figure of the guy I know as Joe is moving, his body shaking as he wanks, his arm pumping hard. I can just hear the odd muffled moan from him, I know he's not going to last much longer. The rose bushes watch on impassively, showering us with their scent, cloaking us in a musk that will always make me think of fucking. There's the smell of disturbed grass too, sharp and astringent, with a ripple of mud and dank earth, which makes me feel connected to the world in a way that never happens during the day. I feel so primal here, the cool breeze whipping at my exposed arse and dangling tits as they dance back and forth with the momentum of coupling.

I am full, I am being fucked and I feel completely alive and that little niggle at the back of my mind that at any moment we could be caught makes it all the better.

Grant squeezes my waist and bangs harder into me, he is about to come. I wish I could reach between my thighs and see to myself, I've been so close to orgasm for so long it would surely take only a flick or two of my finger to allow me to come, but I focus on the pleasure emanating from my pussy, I can always frig myself before sleep. His thrusts are harder, deeper and more ragged. He shifts his grip, moving higher up my body, under my top to just over my shoulders. He holds me in his grasp, his fingers digging in as he moans then, as if a rope inside him has snapped, he scratches his nails down my back and holds himself deep within me. I scream out in pain, in shock and in complete and utter submission. My body shakes with built-up lust and the tracks of his fingernails throb in time with the eager milking of my pussy.

My eyes close as the pleasurable pain rips through me and when I open them again Joe is gone. No surprise there. Grant strokes my back and pulls out of me. I wait until he's moved back from me then I lean back on my haunches, let my skirt settle, then stand. I feel rigid and cold. It is time for me to go home, to wank and to sleep. I don't normally hang around to say goodbye, so once I stuff my tits back in my top I start to walk off towards the park gates.

'Hey, Carrie, wait for me.' I turn around as Grant comes up behind me and slips an arm around my shoulders. I hiss as a sharp throb reminds me of the nail trails there. 'Oh, sorry. I didn't mean to get so carried away.'

'It's OK,' I reply, 'I liked it.'

'Yeah, so did I.' He's blushing, I can see his pale cheeks shining red as we get closer to the streetlights.

'Look, Grant, it's late and I should really be getting home.' I had definitely enjoyed fucking Grant but I don't think this is a date and I don't want him to think that either.

'Oh, I know, I'll walk with you. It's late, you never know who could be hanging around.' He winks and laughs. I can't help myself. So I give in and let him keep his arm around me as we walk onto the street. It is feeling colder now and his body heat is appreciated. We don't speak, we just walk. I only live a little way from the park and we soon find ourselves on the pavement outside my house.

'OK, so it was … erm, lovely seeing you again.' I shuffle from foot to foot. This is why I don't do conventional dating. I'm crap at all the practical stuff.

'And it was lovely fucking you –' Grant smirked '– but you didn't come, did you?'

My brow crinkles with confusion. 'Well, no, I didn't, not so to speak but I enjoyed it though and –'

He kisses me, takes me totally of guard and manages to Snd t I push me back against the lamppost. I wonder what he's doing but his lips on mine distract me and I find myself falling into the kiss, passion re-igniting and once more I'm aware of my damp thighs and sex-swollen pussy. Grant runs his hand down from my waist over my little skirt and then under it. I gasp and lift my arm, pull on his arm. It's one thing to fuck in the dark of the park but under the streetlight? Anyone could see. My neighbours could see.

'Stop,' he says and nibbles my neck, 'let me make you come.'

'But –'

'The quicker you agree, the sooner you come, all this fuss and fluster stops. If you keep on protesting who knows who will come out and see you here with a guy's hands up your skirt like a common prostitute.'

Shit, he knows just how to manipulate me and I love it. I want to be his whore so I let go of his wrist and wrap my arms around his shoulders. He pushes his fingers between my thighs and dips the tips in my juices. He slips between the folds and grazes over my clit. I gasp and bury my head in his shoulder as the pleasure radiates through me. I'm letting him fingerfuck me outside my own home in the glaring light of the streetlamp. It isn't like the thrill of the dark rose bed: it's more intense, more urgent. Someone could walk past at any moment and we'd be discovered.

I tense up as I hear the motor of a car; it's coming towards us. He doesn't stop, even when I dig my fingers into his shoulders and hiss at him to stop. He doesn't, but neither does the car and as the drone of it disappears I relax into his arms again, the adrenaline still pumping through my veins and pushing me closer to climax. I pant and groan, writhe and gasp as the rubbing of his fingers becomes all too much for me. I think I'm going to fall, I think I'm going to explode but then the orgasm hits and I clamp my thighs around his hand and cling on as ecstasy washes through me. I can't think, can't move, I am just rolling along on the waves of pleasure. Grant pulls his fingers away from me and brushes down my skirt.

'Now you can go home to bed.' He smiles and I reach up to kiss him in my appreciation.

'Want to come with me?' I ask, holding him close.

'Can you manage that again so soon?' He cups my face with his hands and I can smell my musk on him. It is intoxicating.

'I won't know if we don't try,' I reply, eager to get him to comply and follow me into my home.

'Well in that case then, I will have to come in just to help you out.' Grant lifts away from me, grabs my hand and pulls me towards my front door.

***

It is weird, going home with the stranger you met in the park for a quick shag. It is strange to compare the thrills of being spanked and fucked in the dark to being tied down and teased on a bed. There is nothing to match the thrill of being naughty in public, coming under a streetlamp like a common whore for example, but you know, when you've found the guy who hits all the right spots you can come anywhere. I thrash and scream as he licks me out, tied spread-eagled on my bed for his pleasure. I sob as he pulls away, denying me just before my orgasm hits. He controls me and I love it and when he finally fucks me, thumbing my clit so I can come around his cock I realise I have found the perfect freak-geek to take out with me to the park. I will never be left disappointed again.

The Arrangement
Cèsar Sanchez Zapata

The rain stopped moments before the black Lincoln Town Car drew to the kerb outside the Hotel Sofitel St James on Waterloo Place. A swarm of people scurried past on the footpath, wielding brollies of different colours and sizes, some lugging briefcases, others rolling wheeled caddies, all of them skipping puddles. Sparkling pools gathered on the pavement, reflecting the rich moonlight and casting its glow over Belinda's face.

To Marshall, she looked magnificent. For a moment he felt the tightness in his chest like adoration, more likely a fleeting hesitation. She gazed out through the window, peering at the white column facade, and in that wondrous instant, he saw the girl he'd married ten years ago.

He watched her a while longer, noting her twitching cheek, her hands fiddling with her handbag. The hem of her skirt rode up her thigh when she crossed her legs, fidgeting as well. She'd spent close to fifty pounds on this dress for the evening. She aimed to make an impression.

Marshall knocked back his Scotch. He placed his hand over her forearm, squeezing gently. She jumped slightly at his touch, turning to face him and smiling after a beat, more for his benefit than anything else.

'You good, honey?' he asked her, his voice soothing and compassionate.

'Grand.'

'Are you cold, then?'

'No, it's fine. The evening's quite refreshing, actually.'

'Right. Well, I can have the driver walk you to the door.'

'That won't be necessary, I don't think.'

He tightened his grip on her arm ever so lightly. 'Are you positive you want to go through with this?'

She nodded. 'I really am.'

They locked eyes and for the time their stare lasted, neither of them spoke. Then she leaned forward, kissed him on the cheek and as she did, she crushed her body right against him, nestled her breasts on his arm. He inhaled the fragrance of her perfume from the nape of her neck, as delicate an aroma as the rest of her. He drowned in the scent, let himself become intoxicated by it. He very nearly snatched her up and kissed her hard on the mouth and ripped the expensive dress to ravage her right then. To hell with the arrangement. Her lips moved inches from his ear, tickling him and her whisper was as soft as a petal drifting in the breeze.

'Don't fall in love with her.'

Then she was gone out the door, high heels tapping on the concrete like the cadence of a coming queen. He observed her as the porter flung open the hotel door, then she was truly gone, disappeared inside the bright lobby bustling with people.

He poured himself another Scotch on the rocks. Macallan's. Fine mark.

He shot that one down also, just as the car door opened and in slipped a woman as stunning as she was sensual. She wore a long, black dress, hugging her hips and her arse like a marvel, and with a slit running down her left side, revealing one sultry leg, smoothed and tanned to perfection.

Marshall had met this woman only once, the night before. Sandra Wellington – the name rolled off the tongue like something wicked and lewd. In fact, that had been his immediate impression of her, sitting at the candle-lit bar in a dress made to clinch her figure most erotically, framing her curves with an opulence that dried his throat. She'd seemed perfectly suited for the cool ambience of Amaya, a restaurant chic and glamorous and exotic enough to be a staple for the rosewood decor. She was older than Marshall [thamay. How much older was relative really when her eyes harnessed a confidence millions of years ahead of him. In her presence, he was acutely aware of that deep-seated feeling inside him of inexperience, something as familiar as grade school arithmetic, perhaps. That sense he remembered from his days at St Agatha's preparatory. He smiled inwardly. That notion of the unknown, of this woman being his guide, his teacher – turned him on incredibly.

'Care for a drink?' he asked her.

'Would you treat a harlot to a drink if she climbed into your vehicle?'

That, too, spawned the rapture in his chest he'd not experienced in years. The sweet, brimming anxiety of something quite unexpected and different, something wholly alien to him. The experience of it was the only lesson to glean, and pleasure happened now to be, as it always was, the prime lesson.

'I think I just might,' he said. 'Champagne to your liking?'

She smiled at Marshall, a smile he likened to a snake preparing to feed.

'I'd love a glass.'

* * *

Almost immediately upon entering the hotel, Belinda was cornered by a round concierge with horn-rimmed glasses and a hideous toupee. He had a quiet intensity that made him seem somehow more alive and buoyant than anyone else around him, and it appealed to her at once. 'Ma'am, can I be of any assistance?' he asked her, and she had but to say the name of the man she was meeting. He ushered her through the high-ceilinged lobby with haste, past crowds of people and a pianist playing 'Sheep May Safely Graze', a harpist regaling in the Rose Lounge, and finally to the St James Bar where she was handed off to a prim maître d' who spoke in an effeminate whisper and gesticulated excitedly with his hands.

The bar was a sophisticated and stylish affair, decked richly in black and red lacquer. The man she had come to see was sitting in a black leather armchair set in a quiet corner beyond the fireplace. He smiled when she arrived before him, and immediately rose from his seat. He was a good deal taller than her, and she fancied that about him; she preferred her men tall and dashing, both qualities this man possessed in spades. He was dressed impeccably, befitting his age, in a three-piece suit of herringbone tweed. No younger bloke could possibly pull off the same look without coming across foppish.

'Belinda, my dear,' he said, his words flowing like honey one upon the next. 'I'm delighted you could join me.'

'Have I kept you waiting long?'

'I'd wait two lifetimes for an audience with you, my dear.'

She smiled as a teenage girl might, and for that smile,

she felt instantly embarrassed, so she blushed. His smile never wavered. It was a knowing smile, a worldly smile. He leaned forward in his chair.

'There's no reason to be nervous, luv. This, you see, is our moment of grace. We speak freely now; we speak at length, we say nothing of direct importance and verbalise everything else, regretting not one syllable.' He took another gulp of his drink, signalling the waiter. 'I've no intention of biting, Belinda. That, I'll only do when you are good and ready.'

One thought sprung to mind upon first beholding Kirkland Wright. He epitomised precisely what Belinda had imagined when reading of Lord Henry Wotton all those years back in grade school. Wotton was merely a creation of Oscar Wilde's, of course, and the perfect dandy had painted Wotton as a young man to boot, yet Belinda had always deemed him a gentleman of age, of [n ore good decadent wisdom. A man of that brand, that unbridled with his desires, with his immoral view of reality, was refined and he had glutted of the world enough to intimately understand that which got his heart racing so rapidly he felt on the verge of faint and set his blood boiling through his veins. In that sense, this man was both Wotton and Dorian Gray, a modern version, cultivated of the latter part of the twentieth century. What truly struck Belinda most about Kirkland was his proclivity for employing words as an extension of his prick. When he talked to a woman, he made love to her; he devoured her mind and her body in a single effort.

There are men devoid of natural filters, who express thoughts without clearly formulating them in their heads, much less considering consequences. Kirkland was of a dying breed that had no use for filters; he knew full well what turmoil his words could reap in a woman – and he didn't care. Not a man you wanted to disappoint with naïveté.

'I've reserved a table in The Balcon,' he said. 'I do hope you're hungry.'

'Famished,' she replied, in a timbre much subdued. 'But what I crave isn't on the menu.' She bent forward, fully conscious of her breasts, and how fabulously they projected forth. 'You have the room prepared, I presume?'

***

The Deluxe Suite he'd booked, Belinda guessed, went for over a thousand quid easy. The design was surprisingly contemporary, stylistically a blend of British traditional with a French flair that was altogether masculine regardless of its nationality. Shades and tones of cream, deep browns, and black lacquer abounded. She ventured inside ahead of him, moseying slowly, sensually, to the centre of the living room. She let his gaze roam over her body, letting him soak her up with his voracious eyes.

'What were your last words to him?' he said.

'I reminded him not to fall for her. Easier said than done, I imagine.'

He pondered a moment, still quietly watching her. 'You married young, did you?'

'Straight out of the university. Blind and stupid. Married in haste, repent at leisure.'

'But very much in love.'

'Oh, yes. I was mad for him. I still am.'

He grabbed the phone from the desk by the window. 'I'll order us up some room service. Make yourself at home.'

She moved listlessly into the bedroom, running her hands across the mattress and the canopy of the four-poster bed. She walked to the lavatory with his eyes following her gentle sway. She turned the silver knob to fill the bathtub. Within a minute it was nearly ready.

***

The driver manoeuvred the car with no clear destination for miles, until suddenly Sandra bobbed in her seat, ordering him to stop and pull the car over. She climbed out and Marshall followed without question. There was a large fenced-in park directly in front of them, the kind nestled in the entrails of a residential building, luxurious and pricey by the looks of it. She fired him a wink that said it all, and promptly, with the ease of a gymnast, hopped the steel gates to the garden on the other side.

They walked down a narrow path overlain with colourful Spanish tile, saying very little, instead stealing fervent caresses and kisses, fleeting yet absolutely deadly, as if carrying on some animalistic mating ritual. A massive, stone fountain centred the communal allotment. It was a lovely structure, tapered with mosaics and patterns at the base and wi [e be fthin the bowl.

Sandra draped her arm around his neck and she kissed him passionately, drawing on the same breath of fresh air from his lungs until there was nothing left for him but to gasp and mumble incomprehensibly. She fixed her hand firmly on his crotch, working him into a state of erection which made him feel, alas, reborn. The fire coming off of her was suffocating, yet he couldn't break away, not for one moment. It was she, in the end, who must have felt his reticence and finally prised herself from his grasp.

'Forgive me. I was under the impression that this was our arrangement, Marshall.'

'I suppose I always thought this sort of thing was strictly for homeless trollops or working-class doggers, pissed on Carlsbergs and apt for a shag behind the corner pub. I never dreamed of having it outdoors.'

'Don't be daft,' she said, laughing. 'There's nothing like it to get the motor running.'

She pulled up her skirt, reaching her hand in and

squirming her underwear down her long, slender legs. She played the elastic bands on her fingers, sashaying her wondrous backside to a bench off the path.

'I'd be mindful if I were you,' he said. 'There's animals roaming about this time of night.'

'That's the idea, my boy.'

He sprung for her, grabbing her waist from behind and forcing her over the back of the bench seat. He raised her skirt clear over her arse, feeling in the darkness for the moist lips of her sex. He licked the taste off his fingers, licked at the excitement that poured from her. Then, whipping his trousers off in a fit of mania, he gripped his engorged cock and he fed it into her pussy. He moved back slightly and let her fit the head of his prick over her pussy, rubbing it across the tiny, dribbling mouth and then nudging her swollen clit. Finally, when neither of them could take any more, she placed him just where he needed to be, then they both trembled from the angst and they exhaled the tension in their bodies, as he was pulled in, like gravity almost, through her tender folds. He slipped slowly inside, centimetre-by-centimetre, deeper and deeper, until she could accommodate no more of him.

He left his cock burrowed within her a moment, doing nothing more than feeling the rapid palpitations of her body clenching at his shaft. Slowly, again, he began to move back and forth, in and out of her sopping wet sex. And he sped up, gradually, to which she met his every thrust with a savage backward thrust of her arse. They reached their peak tempo in the snap of a finger because, first and foremost, it's what they each sought from the other, nothing soft, nothing affectionate; they hungered for the ferocity lying hidden beneath the surface of their cool exteriors. They needed to unleash that fury, and they needed the release more than anything in the world. They slammed into one another with all the grace of two charging bulls. He grasped her tightly by her haunches and he drove forward and pulled back.

'My tits,' she gasped. 'Squeeze them, please! Choke the life out of them!'

He kneaded the soft flesh tightly and squeezed the nipples hard, and felt her shudder, every inch shaking from pleasure. Her body froze and went perfectly rigid, just before his own dam burst and he shot off inside her, every drop of hot, sticky passion gushed into her deepest realm from his throbbing prick.

'Bloody hell!' He rolled to his left, depleted, and his body sore through and through. 'That was bleeding deadly, Christ almighty!' They died at that moment, in each other's arms, the way the best fucks in the world leave you feeling one step from the grave. From somewhere [romembl in that murky consciousness, he glanced up to see the faces of no less than a dozen people peering out their windows, older and proper folk peeping the show.

'Looks like we've managed to rouse an audience. We'd better get on before one of them calls the coppers.'

'Oh, I wouldn't worry. They're positively harmless. They won't do a thing.'

He tugged up his pants. 'Why's that?'

'I own the building,' she said, snickering at her private joke. 'You mustn't be rude, Marshall. Wave to my neighbours. Occasionally, I enjoy putting on a little show for them. Breathe a little life back into the poor saps, you know?'

* * *

Belinda undressed with the door wide open behind her and with Kirkland standing just outside, removing his tie, unbuttoning his shirt. He hung up the phone, kicked off his shoes. She felt his eyes gorging themselves on the sight of her luscious body, feasting on her bare arse as she slipped, leisurely, into the tub. The instant she was in, her tensions washed away. He walked in, now completely naked, his penis waving rigid in front of him.

'It's a wonderful prick,' she said, dreamily, her body overwrought with feverish tremors.

He sidled over to her, so the tip of his cock nearly grazed her cheeks. She gripped it with her hand, stroking it gingerly at first, gauging his reaction, then grasped it tight with both hands and jerked him faster. He grunted his delight. Her beautiful eyes flashed up at him before she circled her tongue over the purple and swollen head. He held her head gently, fingers tangling in her long hair, guiding her movements as she worked her lips over the crown, sucking in her cheeks and massaging his balls. He reached down, thrusting his prick so far in her mouth Belinda could almost feel him in her throat. His long, thin fingers submerged and found her clit.

He fondled her honey pot affectionately, as if petting a furry kitten with one finger, then two, now one again. He was really quite good at it, delicious even. She wasn't extremely hairy down there, well, Marshall favoured that bit of overgrowth, but wet from the bath and the nectar creaming through her gaping pussy, he twirled his palm over the matted down. Fuck it, thought she, if what he wants is a feline, then I'll give him one. She purred and hissed whenever he rubbed the tiny nub that set her off. She nibbled on the tip of his cock, feeling him quiver. When her climax hit, she bared her fangs, dug them in deep at the root of his prick. His hips bucked, three times rapidly, oh, oh, oh! And he squirted thick, white strands of cum across her eye, her nose and mouth. She sank back into the tub, exhausted, merry – and yes, when the lull swept her over that way, she was positively meowing.

***

The driver was waiting with the door held open when Sandra and Marshall emerged from the shadows of the park. She slipped in easily, almost in a crawl, hiking her arse in the air so her skirt rode up and revealed she'd nothing on underneath.

'Give us a few minutes,' said Marshall, tucking a fifty pound note into the man's pocket. 'And slip in the ear plugs if you have them handy.'

'Yes, sir. Absolutely, sir.'

The driver shut the door behind Marshall. Immediately, he was overwrought with the smell of her sex, of their sweat and musk. There never was an aroma as powerful. He reached for her in a hurry, and she slapped his hand away. He tried for her again, and twice more.

'Now, listen here, I [ist.'< won't take any more of your soft screwing,' she said. 'You save that for your little lady. Me – you devour, understand? You give me all of it, or none of it. No restraints!'

He got a hold of her finally, burying his hand between her legs, breathing hard into the side of her face. Her body squirmed restlessly.

She rubbed against him, freeing his cock through the fly of his trousers. 'For me, you pull out all the stops.'

Effortlessly, he lifted her by her firm, smooth haunches, and thrust his prick in, sank it all the way to the hilt. He toppled her onto the seat and without further deliberation he was set off full of sound and fury. Before long, she was pleading with him, with the most blatant disregard for propriety and demureness, to keep it up, or if he were capable, to give her more! All in the Queen's English. Never disengaging, as if the very thought of being severed from his pecker was impossible, she raised herself on her knees, sinking her face into the leather seats, arse poised high and wriggling hysterically. She moved her hands down between her thighs, stroking her clit to alleviate the burning there. She wanted the absolute works, and by God, if he didn't give it to her.

That time it was wild and it was savage. More so than their session in the park, out in the open, him screwing into her like she were a bitch in heat, and her barking at the moon like one. In no time, almost immediately in fact, she mounted a memorable climax, then a second, and Marshall thought perhaps another soon after that, but he couldn't be certain. She felt him tighten like a coil, and she shoved him off, then, gripping him right by the staff, she guided him into her asshole, twisting that sizzling backside to gobble each and every inch.

It was too much, far too much.

He watched her dip her hand into the pool of white cum, coiling the tip of her index finger, and using that to frig herself to another orgasm. He'd never met a woman that was truly insatiable, and now, he thought, he finally had. He stuffed his prick back into his pants, then climbed out of the limo. The driver offered a devious grin, and gratefully accepted another tip from Marshall.

'Aren't you riding back with me?' she asked from inside.

Marshall shook his head, no. 'I have a different arrangement.'

She nodded, tugging the skirt down her legs. 'It was blissful, Marshall. One for the books. I shall never forget you.' She blew him a kiss, and settled into the seat. 'Have yourself a good night, baby.'

'Give my regards to Kirkland.'

'Will do.'

The car lurched forward and before long it disappeared around the corner streetlamp.

* * *

Fresh from a scalding hot shower, Kirkland emerged to find Belinda on the comfy chair and ottoman by the open window, stretched out like a lazy cat. He knelt at her feet and grasped both of her breasts in his large hands. His fingers worked over the stiff, rose-tipped nipples and he kissed each after twisting them rough enough to make her squeal and squirm.

He eased her back and raised her legs in the air. He placed his hands behind her knees, running his tongue down the cleft of her pussy, all the way down between the succulent globules of her arse. Planting a firm, wet kiss on them as well, he pushed her thighs wide apart, revealing her pussy lips puffed-up and red with anticipation. With his fingers, he parted the folds, exposing her twitching pink rose.

His fingertips burrowed into her pussy, assaultin [sy,hisg the tiny nub at her apex, stroking it hard and fast. He played his lips on the inside of her thighs, his breath warm, as if he were whispering, humming all that he planned to do with her. He dug the heel of his palm against her, pressing hard circles around the soft lips of her sex, pressing them deep into her. She twisted beneath him once his tongue had started in on her. She felt the vibrations all the way to her chest, feeling her every muscle turned rigid from the pleasure; her hand tightened on his hair, nails scratching at his scalp. She reached above to grab the back of the chair, steading herself, mouth open and gasping, breathing rapidly as her orgasm drew ever closer.

'Sir?'

'Yes, luv.'

'I'm ready now,' she said.

'Are you certain?'

She reached down and seized his prick, and in her palm it grew large and stiff. She liked the look and feel of it very much; with it, she was sure, she could do wonders. 'You mustn't make me wait another second.'

***

The sky had turned an obscure orange outline over the canopy of trees. Marshall sat on a wooden bench perched on a small hill approximately fifteen feet from the walking trail.

Belinda arrived soon after the birds started chirping. She'd crept onto the seat beside him before he realised she was there. They smiled, genuine smiles, exhausted smiles, and they kissed quickly on the lips, a peck no less imbued with affection and love. But otherwise, there was nothing. No questions. She squeezed into Marshall's side, and he lifted his arm over her shoulders. They neither spoke nor offered anything else. There was very little to say by way of explanation of the evening.

That was, after all, the arrangement.

Together, they stared at the sun rising higher in the sky.

www.ingramcontent.com/pod-product-compliance
Ingram Content Group UK Ltd.
Pitfield, Milton Keynes, MK11 3LW, UK
UKHW022300180325
456436UK00003B/160